SACRED SECRETS OF THE CEDAR CHEST

ANGELA PISATURO

WESTBOW
PRESS®
A DIVISION OF THOMAS NELSON
& ZONDERVAN

WestBow Press books may be ordered through booksellers or by contacting:

WestBow Press
A Division of Thomas Nelson & Zondervan
1663 Liberty Drive
Bloomington, IN 47403
www.westbowpress.com
1 (866) 928-1240

ISBN: 978-1-9736-1371-8 (sc)
ISBN: 978-1-9736-1373-2 (hc)
ISBN: 978-1-9736-1372-5 (e)

Library of Congress Control Number: 2018900192

Print information available on the last page.

WestBow Press rev. date: 03/08/2018

For Mom,
Be at peace in heaven.

This novel, while containing true-to-life situations, is a work of fiction. The story is a collective portrayal of the daily routine in a household where there is someone suffering from bipolar disorder.

The author wishes to bring awareness of the complexity of mental illness and its bearing on each sufferer and their families, as the severity of the disease varies from each individual.

The story is not intended to criticize the sufferer for their illness, or draw empathy for the caregivers and family members, but to leave the reader with one basic truth; that there isn't any circumstance, disorder or destructive behavior so hopeless that the grace of God, and his mercy cannot overcome, bringing about a healthier life for all involved.

All things are possible with God, especially the restoration of broken lives and broken homes.

PROLOGUE

My sapphire eyes can break down anyone; Criminal, Colleague, or your own Grandmother. There's nothing that gets passed me, and I'm proud of that fact. In this business you have to get the story, no matter how it's obtained, or else the world, including your colleagues, will call you an amateur.

I'm a reporter for Heritage World News in Rhode Island. I'm proud of my work and I intend to stay in this position, whatever it takes. I will not be reduced to a menial job at some boring corporation—that's for people who have no imagination, and no life.

Experience has taught me to dig deep to find the real dirt of a story and expose the lies, regardless of whom they may hurt. You ask what is truth?

Truth is different things to different people. There are those who think there are absolutes, but I tell you, if it's your truth, hold onto it at all costs. In my world that's how I roll–take it or leave it, that's your choice.

CHAPTER ONE

"So there you have it, Rhode Islanders. The so-called 'Good Samaritan' woman who opened up her home to unwanted kids had an ulterior motive. That's right folks! Miss Margaret Beecher was a fraud. She used her foster kids as free labor for her illegal import and export business. Authorities have not yet disclosed the nature of that business, but when they do, you will hear it first from Veronica Wheaton.

It seems these kids have slipped through our wonderful system again! Are you as outraged as I am? This is Veronica Wheaton reporting for WJTM, Rhode Island saying, good night and good luck!"

"Cut!" Veronica shouted to the cameraman, her piercing sapphire eyes glaring as she walked over to him. Leonard fidgeted, chewing on his finger nail, his face flushed red.

"So what bug crawled up your pants?" Veronica's voice sounded as shrill as chalk on a black-board.

"No-nothing, nothing's crawled..." The young intern's voice shook with every word.

"So go ahead and tell me that I'm a big bully for being so blunt to the entire WJTM audience!" Veronica stared him down.

"I, I wasn't going to say anything," he said as he slowly backed away from her.

"Let me enlighten you about being an ace reporter, you need to tell the cold, hard facts. You can't dance around the truth, because that won't cut the mustard."

"I, I just think maybe you should…." Leonard said as he gulped.

"I should what, Lenny boy, spit it out!" she snarled as she backed him into a corner.

"Should have waited until all the reports from the police were confirmed? " Leonard pulled at his hangnail.

Veronica let out a milk-curdling laugh. "Is that what you think?"

"Ye, yes, I do. That's what we were taught in school."

"Well, is that so? Let me enlighten you to something, school doesn't teach squat about how to deal in the real world. But don't sweat it, kid. I'll toughen you up." Then Veronica turned around, her eyes spewing fiery darts, causing the rest of the news staff to inch away from her.

"What a bunch of wimps! How do any of you expect to become something, if you're afraid of your own colleague?" she shouted as she slithered away.

Veronica learned that lesson the hard way when she was a rookie, just starting out in the business. She believed the bleeding–heart story a young father told her about his wife, and how she had taken the children, and ran away, when, in reality, he had killed them all, burying them in an open grave at the cemetery in another state.

At the time, the investigation was still underway, and Veronica's reporting and interviewing of the husband influenced his acquittal. She promised herself she would never be that stupid again.

"This case is different. I'm smarter now and not so easily taken in by a good sob-story." She went over the process that she followed for this current case in her mind. Yes, she had done a thorough job of checking the facts, except for the facts her new intern, Marcy had dug up, but she taught her well, Marcy knew what to do. "I feel confident of the accuracy regarding the research Marcy conducted. An intern will never learn if they're babysat all the time. The kid has what it takes to make it in this business." Veronica reflected for a moment. "Someday Marcy will be as good as I am, but I'm not going to tell her that and give the kid a big ego. As a matter of fact, Marcy even looks a little bit like me; beautiful eyes, fetching body, gorgeous hair. I know I'm just a sight to behold on the camera and Marcy will also be one day, if she pays close attention to how it's done."

Veronica finished her report and pushed the 'send' button to ensure Mark, her boss, received it at close of day, so he could review it before her morning broadcast. She then shut off her computer, grabbed her purse and briefcase and walked out of the office toward the elevators. Mark was behind closed doors on some conference call, and most of the staff had already left for the day.

Veronica felt she did an outstanding job covering today's story and decided to reward herself by leaving the office at six, instead of her usual past seven. At home she planned on pampering herself by taking a warm, soothing, bubble bath and opening that new bottle of wine she had purchased yesterday.

As she walked into the elevator, she heard Marcy calling after her. Veronica held the door open with her hand for Marcy to enter.

"Well, if it isn't my ace reporter. What are you still doing here on a Friday night?" Veronica patted Marcy on the back.

"I waited for you because I wanted to tell you that I saw that entire ugly thing. Those idiots, you're the best in the business. If they had half a brain they'd see that. I just wanted you to know that I don't agree with them." Marcy's eyes lit up as she spoke. Veronica sucked in all the adoration.

"You're going places, Marcy. Someday, you'll be working right alongside me."

Marcy's eyes grew wide, "Do you really think so?"

"I know so. Now have yourself a good holiday weekend and I'll see you on Tuesday."

"Thanks, Veronica. I'm so thrilled to be here working with you."

As Veronica walked out of the elevator and toward her car, she whispered to herself, *sure you are kid; who in their right mind wouldn't be thrilled to work with me?*

As Veronica started the engine to her Jaguar, she thought about the upcoming Fourth of July weekend. Everyone in the office had plans for family cookouts and fireworks celebrations, except for her.

Roy, the station's weatherman, had invited her to his barbeque, but she didn't want that bible thumping, scripture spouting knit–wit, preaching at her. She knew that's the only reason why he invited her. "I'm his 'save–a–soul' project. *The guy thinks he's Jesus.*" She pulled out of the station's parking lot and onto the service road that led to the highway.

Veronica thought back on her youth. She believed in Christ once, but that was before her father left her alone with that *crazy mother* of hers, who nearly destroyed her life. She had prayed and begged God to return her father to her, but it never happened. "If my dad, who was everything I admired and trusted, left home, how could I trust in a God I never met and who doesn't care if a kid is hurting?"

The past had a way of rearing its ugly head every now and again. Therapists called them 'triggers', things that stir up old dirt. Yes, she saw a Therapist once. However, he was so busy trying to convince Veronica she needed to take responsibility for her feelings, instead of blaming everyone else, that she left the session one afternoon in a fit of anger, never to return.

"Digging up old dirt, that's what I'm about. I suppose it's just who I am—what colors my world, what makes me tick."

Veronica pulled into the driveway of her townhome. Except for her morning news report, she'd be alone with nothing to do this weekend. She was starting to regret not accepting Roy's invite and that troubled her; why should she care about being at that barbeque, of all places. She would rather have a root canal.

But, in the back of her mind, she always carried the fear that someday she would turn out just like her mom and go crazy.

She shook the ugly notions away, and thought of what to do in order to keep busy over the long weekend.

"Maybe I'll rent a good movie, or go to the beach. Perhaps see the fireworks display over the harbor, or clean out that closet I've been wanting to clean. I don't like those celebrations, they always remind me of when I use to celebrate with Dad. Maybe I'm better off alone; these things cause so much pain, it's not really worth the effort in the long run."

Veronica undressed, then drew a warm lavender-scented bubble bath in the four-claw tub. The bubble bath helped to release the tension she felt in her muscles.

Afterwards, she sat in the loveseat that faced the large bay window and gazed out at the harbor. In the distance, she could see the mansions at Newport as pleasure cruisers rippled in the water; even in the moonlight, the stately mansions shone and some of them belonged to the rich and powerful.

"Someday I'll own a mansion with servants. Then nobody will make me feel small again."

She drifted into thought once more, this time to one particular Fourth of July–the last Fourth she ever cared to celebrate. She was eight years old, and Mom had just come home from the hospital after suffering another bout with depression.

For the first time, Veronica was old enough to understand what had happened. Scenes of a struggle between her mother and father played out in her head. "Eleanor, give me that thing before someone gets hurt!" Ben shouted as he fought to free the knife from her.

"No! Leave me alone." Eleanor's shrill voice filled the air, sending a chill down Veronica's spine.

"What about Veronica and me, don't you care about us? What will happen to us if you kill yourself?" Ben's wounded voice made Veronica cry. Then she released her grip on the knife, causing it to fall to the ground.

"Veronica? What's she got to do with this, she's just a kid and you, what a disappointment you both are. You never know what I need, you're so useless!"

"Veronica is your daughter, how can you say that?" Ben's eyes glistened with tears.

"Don't remind me of that. She's just such a disappointment. I see other girls her age, all loving and kind to their mothers, but this one; what a lousy, ungrateful kid!"

Suddenly a dish on top of the China cabinet, crashed to the ground, Veronica came out from behind the cabinet, trembling and crying. Her father ran to her side.

"It's okay, baby. It was an accident."

"But, she'll disown me!"

"No, darling, she won't. I'm here." Ben held his trembling child close to him, but she would not be comforted. She broke free and ran out of the kitchen and into the backyard. As she ran, she heard her mother screaming at her dad, "Didn't I tell you she was no good!"

Ben picked up the knife from the floor, and then bolted out of the house in search of Veronica. He found her up in the tree house in their backyard. He placed the knife on the patio table, and then climbed into the treehouse.

"My sweet baby girl, Mommy is sick and doesn't know what she is doing," His voice trembled as he spoke. Veronica grabbed her father's cheeks with both hands, as her sapphire eyes pierced into his very soul. Now she spoke clearly and deliberately, "Yes, she *does* know what she's doing. Ben wiped a tear from her eye.

Ben appeared wounded by her words. He took Veronica and sat her on his knee, "Yes, there are times Mommy does hurt us on purpose, but it's still part of her disease. Someday when you're older, you will understand that she's not capable of love like everyone else, but she does love you in her own way."

Veronica just stared at her daddy. She did not say another word.

Then Ben spoke again. "Veronica, honey, I'm going to take you next door to Mrs. Morgan's for a while, until Mommy feels better, okay?" Veronica just stared at her father.

Ben cleared his throat and continued to state his case. "You told me you liked her and she always makes those great cookies." He kissed her on the head.

"But, I don't want cookies. It's the Fourth of July and you

promised we would go to see the fireworks at the park." Veronica's eyes grew wide.

"Honey, I'll come home to bring you to the fireworks, I promise you. It will be you and me at the fireworks in the park." He took Veronica by the hand and climbed down from the treehouse.

As they walked over to Mrs. Morgan's place, Veronica wondered if her mother would ever come back. Deep inside herself, where bad children live, Veronica wished she never would.

Perhaps her mother was right. What child wishes her parent to go away and never return?

"Honey, come away from the window, you'll get wet from the sprinklers watering the lawn. They seem to always wet the windowsill for some reason. Your daddy will be back soon," Mrs. Morgan said as she pulled the frightened little girl from the window.

"Let's have cookies and milk. I baked those spice cookies you like so much," Mrs. Morgan held one up.

"See, they're in the shape of the flag and frosted red, white and blue."

Veronica pushed away the tray of cookies that now sat on the table in front of her, "I don't want any of your stupid cookies!"

Mrs. Morgan took the tray and placed it at the far end of the table, then she sighed. "Okay, so what do you want to do this afternoon?"

"I don't know, I just want to go with my Dad."

Mrs. Morgan squeezed her hand. "Poor little thing, so much pain for you at such a young age."

Veronica pulled her hand free; as much as she wanted to ignore the cookies, she couldn't. The sight of them was more than she could resist.

"Well, maybe I'll have one cookie."

"That's a good girl." Mrs. Morgan patted Veronica on the head.

"Would you like to take Missy for a walk with me?"

"Okay, but just for a little while." Veronica took hold of the Beagle's leash and walked down the street with Mrs. Morgan. She laughed at Missy, trying to catch a squirrel, and then they walked on the trail by the park. Missy was so entertaining, Veronica almost forgot she was angry.

As they were walking back to the house, Veronica saw her father waiting on the front steps. She let go of the dog leash and ran straight into his arms. "Daddy, Daddy, you've come back!"

"Hey baby, I told you I would. How was your time with Mrs. Morgan?" He swept her up off the ground and hugged her tightly.

She shrugged her shoulders. "It was okay. The dog is fun."

"Well, that's good to hear." Ben pinched her cheek.

"How's the missus?" Mrs. Morgan gave of look of concern.

"She'll pull through, but it's going to take a while," he sighed.

"Well, that's good news, you're a good man, Ben, don't let anybody tell you otherwise," Mrs. Morgan patted his shoulder.

Ben cleared his throat, "I'm not so sure I'm that good of a man, as you say I am."

"Of course, you are. It's just the pain talking now." She gave him a warm smile.

Mrs. Morgan had no way of knowing that he planned on leaving tonight, bringing his sweet baby girl to her uncle Jeb's to be raised.

Mrs. Morgan waved to Veronica as she left for the park with her Dad. "Enjoy the night, honey," she called after her.

The fireworks were magical. Her father was so attentive and kind. Veronica loved those times when it was just the two of them. Her mother somehow always managed to ruin their fun with her outbursts, embarrassing them in public.

Ben held Veronica close to him as he spoke. "You know Daddy loves you, don't you baby?"

"Sure Daddy, I know that." Veronica detected a tone of sadness in her father's voice.

"Is Mommy making you give me away?" Veronica's glare pierced his soul.

Ben narrowed his eyes. "Why would you ask a question like that?"

"Because she always says God made a mistake when He made me and that I'm not a good daughter, and if I don't make her happy, she'll give me away."

"Oh baby, she doesn't mean those things."

"Yes, she does. I'm not stupid; I know what she means, and what she doesn't!"

"How I wish I could make you understand. Things happen sometimes; life can be cruel. But remember I'll always love you no matter what."

Veronica wondered about her father's behavior. She always knew he loved her. *Why did he have to repeat it tonight when they were having fun?*

"Honey, Uncle Jeb is going to come tomorrow to take you to his house to stay with him for a while, just until Mommy's better."

Veronica put her face in her father's and squeezed his cheeks. "Why? Where are you going?"

"Honey, please it's better this way for now. I'm doing this for you. Uncle Jeb is a good man, and he loves you a lot."

"So why can't he come here to our house to take care of me?"

"Because it will be better for you at his house. I have a lot to do, and I won't have enough time for you, with having to get things ready for Mommy, plus going to work and the hospital."

"So, when you're busy I can stay with Mrs. Morgan."

"Please honey, do this for me."

Veronica put her hands on her hips. "Okay, Daddy, but I don't like it!"

"That's my good girl." Ben gave her an affectionate kiss on the cheek.

That was the last time Veronica heard her father's voice or felt his strong arms around her or felt his sweet kiss on her cheek. Little did she know that night would change her life forever.

CHAPTER TWO

The sunlight streamed across the windowsill, dancing upon Veronica's face, waking her from a deep sleep. She stretched as she sat up in her bed, then headed for the kitchen for a morning cup of coffee. As she sipped the steamy brew, she felt relieved to put the holiday weekend behind her, at least now she could get back to what's really important.

In a moment of weakness the night before, she walked the half mile from her place to the harbor. She hoped that watching the fireworks would help to vanish her dark mood. After dodging excited, screaming children, running around like wild animals, and couples kissing and pawing each other, like two dogs in heat, she had had enough. When she returned home she breathed a sigh of relief, and went straight to bed.

She awoke the next morning to a beautiful, sunny day. Now her life could return to normal. She dressed in her blue suit and blue pumps, with matching purse, she called this her 'power suit', and then drove to the office ready to tackle the Fourth of July tragic stories that undoubtedly filled the newsroom over the weekend.

There always was a rash of incidents; children getting hurt by fireworks, accidents on the docks from those who over-drank; it was a smorgasbord of stupidity.

She parked her car in the V.I.P. spot, exited the car, and sauntered into the office. Veronica wanted to give the impression she was in control, not to mention having had a satisfying weekend, but her plan backfired. She strolled into the newsroom area where the staff gathered the morning news reports, showing off her new designer blue heels.

"Hi everyone, have a good weekend?" Veronica's lack of sincerity was evident.

Then Leonard, the cameraman, and Louise, the editorial assistant, huddled together, whispering what they didn't want her to hear, but she did hear it anyway.

"She's so smug and shallow," Louise's eyes narrowed.

"Yeah, but I hear she's had a rough life," Leonard shrugged.

"Oh please! Who hasn't had a bad life, that's no excuse for her behavior," Louise blew out a breath.

Leonard touched his chin. "She did make that poor woman cry on national television. You know, the one whose son accidentally drowned in their pool."

Louise shook her head. "That's right, I remember that. She nearly ruined that poor family."

"Well, what goes around comes around," Leonard took a sip of his coffee as he perused the copy that came over the fax machine.

"You said it," Louise squeezed his arm.

Veronica's nostrils flared, as she came into view. She'd been berated and torn apart her entire life. Enough was enough.

She approached them as they stood, still chatting at Leonard's desk; her eyes glaring at them, then they turned and noticed her approach.

"So, you two think what goes around comes around, eh?"

"Well, we…" Leonard stuttered.

"Well, the truth is that you're so unkind, Veronica. People try to befriend you, but you push them away," Louise stared back at her.

"It's my prerogative to accept or reject any invitation and you two *motley creatures* have just proven case in point. People are cruel. It's a dog—eat—dog world, so WATCH IT!"

"Look, Veronica, we've all had—"

Veronica interrupted. "We've all had what? We've all been

abandoned by the only person we trusted? We've all been raised in a nut house?" Veronica's voice screeched through the walls, causing her boss to enter the room, but she kept on shouting at her co-workers.

"We've all had our father's break a promise and never return!" Veronica stepped into Louise's space, staring her down.

"Veronica, please step into my office." Mark, her boss said as he walked toward her.

"We're talking here," Her eyes spew fiery darts.

"Veronica, don't push it." Mark glared at her, then he turned on his heels and that was Veronica's cue to follow. He shut the door, and sat down next to her on the sofa.

"Look, I'm talking to you as a friend. You need to chill out, or I'll have to let you go."

"Let me go where?" You know, you're really funny this morning, a regular laugh riot!" Veronica's laugh rang with scorn. *Who does Mark think he is talking to, a common thug? I'm Veronica Wheaton, the best in the industry.*

"Veronica, you need help."

"That's everybody's answer for everything, isn't it? Well, it's this temperament of mine that has made me the best in the industry, and don't you forget it!" Veronica got up from her seat and walked over to the window, still shouting and wagging her finger at him.

Mark took a deep breath, then walked behind his desk, grabbing a folder, and bringing it to the sofa, and then motioning for Veronica to sit next to him. Veronica turned back to look at him, letting out an exasperated sigh, as she took her sweet time getting to the sofa.

"I got this in last night. Seems a mother left her son on the doorstep of a children's village about three months ago in Tarrytown, New York. A note was pinned to his blanket saying, "they are out to get me. Take my child and raise him."

"Another loon on the loose, the world is full of them." she smirked.

"Well, the hospitals were checked and they found out where

baby Ryan was born. Apparently, after that incident, the husband had her committed. You know, the unfit mother thing."

"So why are you telling me about this?"

"This is your next assignment." He spoke in deliberate tones. Veronica rolled her eyes as Mark continued.

"As always there is a twist. Hospital reports confirm there were marks on the mother's body when she arrived at the institution, and they didn't appear to be self–inflicted, but when the police got involved, they deemed it an open and shut case, saying the bruises were indeed, self–inflicted."

"So what do you want from me?" she narrowed her eyes.

"Tarrytown is your hometown, isn't it?"

"Yeah, so what's that got to do with it?"

"Well, this case takes place there, and I want you to go and check out her story. Visit the mental hospital. Visit the Hall of Records for marriage license, baby's birth certificate, etc. You know the drill."

"So you're telling me I have to take this lame assignment? What if I won't?"

Mark leaned in close to her face. "Then, you'll enter into counseling for three months."

"So send me! Let them declare me crazy; I don't really care anymore," she waved her hand in dismissal.

Mark pulled back and spoke in slow, pronounced words. "Veronica, it's away at a clinic. You'll be on extended sick leave."

"Oh, I see, so you want to put me away, as well as have me declared unfit," she stared him down.

"I never said that, but the choice is yours; take the assignment, or take the counseling."

She yanked the folder out of his hand, and then she walked toward the door. "I guess I'm going to Tarrytown. See you in a week," she smirked.

"No, Veronica. I'll see you in three months." Mark held up his hand to silence her.

"Great! I'll send you a postcard!" She shouted back to him as she left the office, slamming the door behind her. She walked at a fast-pace, keeping her head down, as she passed her colleagues on the way to the office exit.

As she headed for the office parking garage, her thoughts ran in every direction. *How could he do this to his ace reporter? He is the one who needs help. I'm his meal ticket. Mark was a loser before he met me.*

Veronica got into her car, and kept driving until she reached the harbor. She sat at the edge of the cliff, watching the waves crash on the rocky shore.

She kept tossing rocks into the water, with each toss, her aim became more forceful, as if she was lashing out at someone, and not just letting out her anger.

"Are you happy, Mom?" she yelled out. "You always said I wasn't going to amount to anything, so you were right after all."

Then she got up and jogged along the jagged cliffs, allowing the warm night winds to cover her face with the mist of the water. Her blood was boiling, and she was about to explode. Crying wasn't an option; only weak people break down.

Her thoughts transported her to an incident when she was a teenage girl; she fell head over heels for the Football Captain. Brent Bishop had been a real hottie, built like an Adonis, sporting olive black eyes that shined in the sunlight and jet black wavy hair. Every girl had wanted him and he had known it. However, as children, having grown up on the same street, they became playmates, and best friends, because of this, Veronica believed he had always loved her.

She believed that all his flattery and tiny pecks on the cheek, and the occasional burger, or ice cream after school with her best friend, meant that he had loved her, even though he had never officially asked Veronica out on a real date until Freshman Homecoming; a fact that somehow eluded her. *After all, they had grown up together on the banks of the Hudson River and played outside her house almost every day.* Then one day at her friend's dare, she had approached him about his intentions. Veronica wore a tight sweater and short skirt showing off her long slender legs. Brent had been standing by his locker when Veronica sauntered up to him. She had placed her hand on his back, patting it gently. "Hi, big guy, what's up?"

"Oh hey, Veronica," Brent continued getting his books from his locker.

Veronica's nostrils flared, "Well, don't look so happy to see me!"

"What are you talking about?" he shrugged.

"Come on, Brent we're a couple, aren't we?"

"A couple...a couple of what?" he laughed.

"You mean all these little kisses and compliments don't mean anything to you? And what about all those after school burgers, and the date for Freshman homecoming. After all we grew up together."

"For Pete's sake, you're such a baby. I liked you once, but things change and now I want to shop around." Brent puffed out his chest like a proud peacock.

"Shop ar...?" Veronica choked up before she could finish the sentence. She had run out of the school, and all the way home, exactly one half of a mile. She ran up to her room and slammed the door. She hadn't even noticed her mother following behind her.

"Veronica, what's your problem now?" Her mother's voice was filled with anger.

"Nothing Mom... just nothing!" tears ran down her cheeks.

"Honestly, why are you so dramatic? Why can't you be like other girls?"

"I know, Mom, I'm a disappointment, poor old you!" Veronica threw herself on the bed.

"So what happened now?" Veronica's mother threw her hands in the air.

"Well, Brent Bishop doesn't want me anymore. I thought he liked me. He told me to get lost, as if you really care!" Veronica buried her face in her pillow and wept.

"You must have done something to make him go away. I mean since nobody wants you, there must be a reason." Her mom's tone of voice was cool and unfeeling; in fact she seemed quite happy her daughter was in pain.

"Yes Mom, you're right, nobody wants me, and you only keep me around for your benefit."

"There you go, twisting my words again. I bet that's why Brent wants nothing to do with you. He is such a sweet boy."

That night Veronica had vowed never to tell her mother anything about her life, deciding to handle everything herself from then on.

Four months later, Eleanor Wheaton had fallen into a deep maniac state, requiring intense therapy in a mental health facility.

Veronica had moved back with her uncle, finishing her last three years of high school in Tarrytown. She had felt like a human volleyball; always being tossed on one side or the other. During this time, she had retreated into a world where she didn't have to feel or think. Her books and her music became her closest friends.

CHAPTER THREE

Veronica was in a trance-like state while driving back home from the harbor. She was so out of it, she wondered how she managed to get there safely; this was not like her. She had always been focused and alert, and this new experience bothered her.

Veronica had spent her entire life, building her loner image and career. She loathed people and the way they would say they were your best friend, or lover, but then leave you without as much as a goodbye. Journalism was her only trustworthy accomplice/companion. She had been unstoppable, until now. *Why now, why the change? Could she be having a breakdown like her mother?*

Veronica entered her condo apartment and noticed the light flashing on her message machine. She walked over to the phone.

"It's probably Mark apologizing for his behavior. After all, he can't do without me," she told herself. She clicked the message button.

"Hey, Veronica, it's Roy; I heard what happened with Mark. I'm sorry, it's a tough break. If you need to talk, call me."

"Sure, you probably want to preach at me about my behavior," she shouted into the phone, as if Roy could hear her.

So, everybody knows Veronica Wheaton, the ace reporter, was spanked today—like nobody else ever made errors in judgment. I suppose I should have double-checked Marcy's facts on that foster care story, but her sources were reliable. Heck, they were my sources.

But, then again, I had allowed her to check out a few tips without my supervision. The kid knew what to do, though. I had trained her, and my methods are indisputable. I'll show Mark I can be a competent reporter again. He'll be sorry he had ever started this Tarrytown ruse.

Veronica poured a glass of red wine, and then turned on the evening news. There on the screen, staring back at her, was her face.

"This late-breaking development from Heritage World News: award winning reporter, Veronica 'stone–hearted' Wheaton, known for her hard-nosed approach to journalism, was given a sabbatical. Our sources tell us that she will be temporarily relocated to Tarrytown, New York, working on a 'alleged' story that will require in–depth investigation. But insiders tell us that the assignment is a last–ditch effort by Heritage World News Editor-in-Chief, Mark McMullen to tame the wild shrew. This is Margo Gentry, saying Goodnight, Newport!"

Veronica sat numb in her seat, the glass of wine slipped from her hand onto the plush, light carpet, but she was too shocked to react.

She knew Mark's assignment was a way to get her out of his hair, but she assumed he'd calm down after she'd come back in a week or so with a good story. But then, there was Roy's message. He was always so dramatic, she hadn't taken it to heart. Now she didn't know what to think. On impulse, she phoned Roy, her fingers trembling, as she punched in his number.

"Hello?"

"Hi, Roy."

"Veronica?"

"Yes, it's me."

"You don't sound like yourself. What's wrong?"

"You tell me, Roy. Am I fired?"

"I don't know. I just know Mark's pretty disgusted with your attitude, not to mention that story you put forth, using your intern's facts, is blowing up in his face. They're saying he's in the business of reporting fake news stories. He wants time to think things through."

"Why didn't he tell me that?" she screamed into the phone.

"Veronica, I can hear you. I'm not deaf."

"Sorry, but what's with him? This wouldn't be the first time his feet were held to the fire."

"Please understand what I'm about to say—" Veronica interrupted before Roy could finish the thought.

"Roy I don't want a religious lecture. Your God doesn't exist for me anymore."

"Look, Veronica, I was going to say you're hard to get through to. You argue about everything. How could he tell you what he was thinking?"

"So I'm hard, huh, what do you think made me a top-notch reporter?"

"Veronica, there's more to reporting than breaking someone's spirit when they've messed up."

"Oh, really? Enlighten me, weatherman."

"Look, you called me for an explanation, remember?"

"Touché."

"This isn't a boxing match; I'm trying to help you."

"I know, I know…"

"You're not going to like what I'm about to say."

Veronica let out a big sigh right into the telephone. "Here we go again."

"I don't care if you don't want to hear it, but I wouldn't be a good friend, if I didn't tell you the truth. So, here goes. You let your shattered childhood color everything you do. You seem to want to make the entire world pay for your bad break in life, and it's not everybody else's fault."

"You don't know my pain, so don't tell me how to feel."

"You're right, I don't; but Jesus does."

"Oh brother!" She shouted so loudly, she almost choked.

"Will you listen to me, just this once? Jesus was abused, his friends abandoned him, the church leaders betrayed him. He didn't deserve it, but you know what he did?"

"No, but I'm sure you will tell me."

"He said to His father." 'Forgive *them; they don't know what they are doing*'"

"Boo, hoo, hoo, you're breaking my heart."

"Your mother wasn't responsible, Veronica. However painful it was for you, forgiveness brings healing."

"I know she hadn't been responsible, but my dad had been!"

"I'm glad to hear you say that. But why do you blame your father?"

"He had promised to return and he didn't." She sniffled.

"Maybe he couldn't. Do you know anything about him, his background and such?"

"No, I don't. He and Mom had always been so secretive about it."

"Well, for an ace reporter you sure have overlooked the most important details of your own family history."

"Okay, so I see your point."

"Why don't you use your time in Tarrytown to retrace your family history? Are there any relatives left?"

"No, he hadn't any siblings."

"Well, there are still county records."

"Yeah, I suppose so."

"One other thing—"

"What now."

"I'm sending you a book. I'd like you to read it. I'll overnight it, so you get it before you leave for Tarrytown."

"I'm not going to read any of it."

"Veronica, give it a shot. You have nothing to lose and everything to gain."

"Fine, W H A T E V E R! Goodbye, Roy."

"Goodbye, Veronica. God bless."

CHAPTER FOUR

The howling winds rattled Veronica's bedroom windows, waking her out of a sound–sleep. She wrapped her robe around her body to keep warm, then walked over to the window seat, that hugged the bay windows, that now were drenched in steady belches of rain.

"Oh great! Are we having a hurricane in this part of the country? Can life get any worse?"

Veronica watched the treacherous winds wreaking havoc across the harbor. The swirling pattern of the wind–blown rain hypnotized her, sending her back into a deep sleep; a sleep that felt like it came from a dark place in her soul.

Suddenly someone's haunting cries filled every corner of the room. Veronica put her hands over her ears, and when that did not work, she placed a pillow over her head, in an effort to block out the sounds, but it was futile; nothing could keep the stirring cries away.

Who is this person in so much pain?

Scenes of her life flashed before her mind's eye. She was six years old, and wandering around in a department store. She saw her mother in the distance, by the cashier. Then someone approached her, thinking she was lost. Even back then, Veronica had found a way to penetrate a human heart to fear or pity with one look.

"Are you lost, sweetheart?" the woman asked, as she touched Veronica's shoulder in a kind and loving manner.

She nodded to indicate she *was* lost, and for dramatic effect, even shed a few tears, to spite the fact that her mother had only been a few feet away.

"Honey, come with me and we'll find your mommy," The kind lady said, as she took Veronica's hand. As the woman walked with her, she said a secret prayer they wouldn't find her mother, and Veronica could go home with the nice lady. Then her mother's shrill voice echoed from the front aisle of the department store, where the cashier stood.

"She belongs to me," and with one swift pull of Veronica's arm, she was back in her mother's grasp. To this day, Veronica could see the horrified look on that woman's face, as she was yanked into her mother's clutches.

She tossed violently, until she awoke in a deep pool of sweat. Suddenly, she was made aware that she was still on the window seat, curled up like a frightened child.

"No! You should have taken me! I wanted to go with you. Why didn't you get the police, lady?" She yelled out to no one.

It had taken her a good ten minutes to calm her nerves. She seemed to be unraveling in bits and pieces over the last few days. The word *manic* was imprinted in her mind.

"I'm not like Mom. She was crazy! This is just a bad memory, nothing more," she shouted out into the empty room.

She went into the kitchen, took a bottle of red wine from her wine rack, and then curled up in an afghan, on the sofa to face the television. Some mindless late–night talk show was on, and it lulled her back to sleep.

Again, she wrestled with the demons of her past, as another scene filled her head. Now she was eight years old, and living with Uncle Jeb in Tarrytown. She wiped an imagery tear from her eye, while she dreamt of that awful night, the beginning of the end, the only unconditional love she had ever known.

"I want my daddy!" She screamed at the top of her lungs, the light from her sapphire eyes, as penetrating as the stars in the night sky.

"Honey, I told you that Daddy is taking care of Mommy." Uncle

Jeb's portly belly pressed against Veronica's chest, as he made an effort to hug her.

"I'm not stupid. I know she's in the crazy hospital!" Veronica's eyes narrowed.

"Your mother is ill, not crazy." Uncle Jeb said, in a tone that sounded like a scolding.

"Yeah, well, you live with her, and then tell me she's not nuts!

"Veronica, we'll talk in the morning, it's time for bed." She walked up the stairs in silence. Veronica knew when her uncle spoke in slow deliberate tones, she was not to push the issue.

Veronica reached the second–floor landing; her uncle on her heels to confirm she went into her room, and not to the next landing and the attic, which she was prone to do at times, to avoid going to sleep. From that vantage point, she could look out the attic window, and watch the moon's glow on the river; there she would pray to God to make her mother normal and loving.

She recalled how good it felt to have the sun shining through the octagon-shaped, stained-glass window, creating patterns of warm color across the wooden attic floor, that reflected on the mahogany bench below it. Veronica loved sitting there and thinking about better days, when her father would come back for her, and they'd be a family again; a family of two.

Veronica chuckled, remembering how Uncle Jeb's belly bounce up and down as he guided her along the red carpeted hallway. Mahogany, brightly polished doors stood at attention from one end of the hallway to another, looking like good little toy soldiers from the "Nutcracker Suite."

After Veronica had calmed down, the Victorian house at Hillcrest Manor became magical. She was the princess, and all the shiny mahogany doors, her subjects. The poster bed with arched canopy, and the rich mahogany doors and window frames became the princess's palace. In the far corner of the room sat a love seat, in the style of King Henry the VIII. The four-poster Mahogany bed had been the vehicle that transported her from place to place, much like the way Cleopatra traveled the countryside.

The best part of all, had been the bay window that faced the Hudson River, where she imagined royal ships passing by and the port, where she had waited for her prince to arrive. As the weeks passed by, Veronica had come to love this magnificent house. She felt loved and wanted here, and it helped her ease the pain of missing her dad.

Veronica's life had become normal again. She actually felt like a little child, with school friends, and parties and all the things that make a kid, a kid. She began to think living here would not be such a bad thing, and she had wanted to stay.

Then Veronica's dream had taken a frightening twist. She was standing at the top of the staircase listening to Millie, Uncle Jeb's girlfriend, and Uncle Jeb whispering; both had worn somber expressions.

The next thing she recalled, had been Uncle Jeb and Millie giving her a cup of tea. Millie had long brown hair, and was as skinny as a pretzel stick, and just as brownish tan in skin tone.

Millie spotted Veronica peeking through the mahogany stairwell and ran up the stairs to her.

"What are you doing hiding in the stairwell, button?" Millie always called her button, and it made Veronica mad.

"Nothing and my name ain't button!"

"I know, it's just a pet name."

"Well, I ain't your pet either!"

"You're a feisty one. How about I tuck you in and tell you a story?"

"How about you tell me what's going on downstairs instead." Veronica said, her haunting eyes staring back at Millie.

"Are you sure you're not more like thirty years old, stuck inside a little girl's body?" Millie quipped, trying to shake the chill she had felt from the child's angry stare.

Veronica just shook her head in disgust. *Why is it that all adults think kids are stupid?*

"It's about my mom, isn't it?"

"Oh no, honey. I—"

"Well, I hope they keep her in that place for good."

"That's a terrible thing to say."

"You live with her, and be her kid, and see if you like it." The front door closed and Uncle Jeb came up the staircase to her room.

"So, what's this all about?" What were you talking about?" Veronica's shrill voice echoed through the room.

"Baby, calm down. We're here; me and Millie, and we love you."

"What's that supposed to mean?" she screamed in her uncle's face.

"Nothing...it means nothing." He swallowed hard.

"Where's my dad?" Veronica's eyes narrowed.

"Veronica, come here, sit on my lap." Veronica pulled Uncle Jeb's beard in such a way, he couldn't move his face.

"You tell me now or else!" She pointed her finger in his face.

"Veronica please... Aren't you concerned about your mother?"

"No! Where's Dad!" No one answered her.

"Where is he?" she shouted out.

"He's gone, honey," Uncle Jeb cleared his throat.

"Gone where?" Crocodile tears fell from her eyes.

"We don't know. He just left us a note."

Now Veronica's screams grew louder and unceasing.

"Please honey, calm down!" Uncle Jeb tried to hold her, but she pulled away.

"No, no! I want my dad!" She ran out into the rain, screaming at the top of her lungs, wearing only her nightgown. Her bare feet slid on the wet grass, causing her to fall on her butt.

"Where are you, Daddy? Don't you dare leave me! I hate you too! Why don't you want me?"

"God, I hate you!" She called out in the night. The next thing she had recalled was that she was wearing dry clothes and Uncle Jeb and Millie, had given her a cup of tea.

After that day Veronica never mentioned her father or God again. The walls around her heart had grown thicker, so that even Uncle Jeb and Millie had struggled to find the Veronica they once had known. The little girl who, for a few short months, had learned to love, had no longer existed, and a monster had taken her place.

CHAPTER FIVE

Veronica's alarm sounded, indicating the start of a new day; a day she had wished was only another nightmare. This was the day she was going to Tarrytown, New York for her new "so-called assignment." Sleep had been non-existent, except for the wild dream-like states that had pledged her during the night. She wasn't in any mood to start a new assignment. *It's more like my worst nightmare and it hasn't even begun.*

Mark had arranged everything in advance. He had booked a suite at the Hudson River Inn for three months, probably because he didn't trust her to make her own reservations, and he would have been right. He also had contacted the Tarrytown Police Department to alert them of Veronica's arrival. He also hoped to get their cooperation, in case she needed any assistance with the case. All the signs were there that Mark had ceased to trust in her judgment as a reporter. *Was she really losing her edge? It can't be so, probably just a lot of stress.*

Veronica entered Interstate I-95S toward Connecticut. She watched pieces of her world go by, first the Newport Harbor with its stately mansions followed by the World Heritage News building where she worked, and right on into Hartford. As she entered I-287 she began to feel smaller than a helpless child.

Then memories began to flood her mind, as her old stomping grounds came into view. She took a deep breath and exited the

Parkway at Hilldale Circle. The hotel sat at the far end of the two-line highway that hugged the Hudson River.

Flashbacks of the ride to Uncle Jeb's, on that fateful day filled her head. She sat alongside her uncle in his blue pickup truck, neither one spoke, as they left her beloved home in Larchmont, New York to go live with him.

On impulse, Veronica pulled away from the hotel and headed for Hillcrest Manor. She went up to the front door, but could not bring herself to go inside. The house seemed lifeless, and almost haunted; a paradox for her childhood life. She meandered around the grounds, taking in the scenery and the salty scent of the river, hoping it would help to build up her courage to enter the house.

Veronica remembered that she had been so nervous that day she left home, she had thrown up. Uncle Jeb was kind though, he pulled over and allowed her to collect herself, never saying a word about it, even though she splattered the passenger side of Uncle Jeb's truck.

They drove up the narrow, unpaved road that led to Uncle Jeb's house on the hill. The majestic house stood on top of that tree-covered hill; now overgrown with vines that rose to the faded paint of the second story. Veronica loved how the second–floor landing had its own porch, and so did the third floor. The windows all had bright blue shutters, now faded by years of neglect. As Veronica stepped onto the front porch, the lose floorboards creaked, it resembled a scene from a horror movie to her.

Now she recalled Uncle Jeb showing her the room; it had been filled with soft pink pillows and an antique poster bed. An array of stuffed animals sat one after the other on the bookshelves, in the south corner, by the painted rocker. This had been a little girl's room, one that hadn't been touched for a long time. Veronica had known that Uncle Jeb had had a little girl who died from influenza at age seven. Her Aunt Lillian, Uncle Jeb's wife, died three years later, some said from a broken heart.

It had felt strange to be in this room. It was so vibrant with life, yet, death hung over its walls like moss on an old stone building.

It was a legacy that had hung over her entire existence at Hillcrest Manor, named by her ancestors after her mother's great, great grandfather, Archibald Hillcrest, who served in Her Majesty's Customs, in England before the family moved to America. It was said that Archibald Hillcrest had suffered from manic disorder, as well, and when he could no longer serve his beloved England, his family moved to Hillcrest Manor. Mental illness had run in her mother's family, a family she so much had disconnected from, a family she had wished was anyone else's, but hers. Her mother's half-brother, Uncle Jeb was the only normal one. Most likely taking after his father's side of the family.

Veronica was made heir to the throne, but had never taken the reins. Hillcrest Manor was not her heritage any longer. She'd made her own heritage: a heritage of one, and she liked it that way.

She stepped onto the rooftop terrace, and looked out onto the horizon. Overgrown willow trees and ferns appeared listless with moss covering their drooping branches, and oak trees that stood bent, as if in mourning, the legacy of a dead existence that was the Hillcrest family.

The condition of the property made her uncomfortable and she thought of leaving for a brief moment, but she didn't feel like going to the Inn just yet.

Three months is a long time. How am I to survive?

She would stay for a while and face the Hillcrest family demons, her own demons. Maybe Roy had a point; it was time to clear the air, and bury the hatchet. What better way than to visit the place that had finally broken her spirit?

Veronica sat on the wingback chair in the corner of the room, and pondered living out of a suitcase for three months, especially in a place she had no desire to be in. Then she took the book Roy had given her, out of her purse. It was small, about the size of a pocket planner book, entitled, *"I Have Loved You with an Everlasting Love."* Veronica skimmed through the book and came across a bible verse: "Jerusalem, Jerusalem, how I longed to gather you under my wings—"

Anger rose on her cheeks like red hot burning coals. "What kind of God would abandon his child, tell me that?" she screamed into nothingness.

Then she threw the book onto the floor, and cried herself to sleep, while the sounds of the Hudson River swished against the jagged rocky shoreline, outside the window.

CHAPTER SIX

Veronica had awakened somewhat disoriented. She rubbed the sleep from her eyes, then scanned her surroundings. She was still in Uncle Jeb's house; *how did that happen?* She ran her fingers over the fabric on the wingback chair, and then it came to her; she had sunk her tire bones into it last night, to read that awful book from Roy. The realization that she had not gone back to the Inn to sleep, frightened, and puzzled her at the same time. *How could she not remember something like that?*

She recalled that at one point she was walking in the night air, trying to shake morbid thoughts free from her mind. Instead of getting a clear head, she wound up more distraught, to the point that she had walked all the way to town, and landed in the Hollow Leg Tavern, where she had drowned her sorrows in a few glasses of wine. She always drank at least two glasses after dinner to relax. *Could she have had too much to drink?*

No, that was impossible. She wasn't a heavy drinker, and she was sure she only had had two glasses at the tavern.

So how'd she wind up here?

Not knowing how to solve this mystery, unnerved her. Maybe she was losing her mind? She shook herself loose from her horrifying thoughts. *I will not entertain such nonsense, there is nothing wrong with my mind; it's a beautiful, intelligent mind, not twisted like my mother's mind.*

She decided to go to the Inn, telling herself to forget this incident. She needed to settle in anyway. But try as she might, her mind wandered back to thoughts of the past night's events, she tried again to shake it lose, but she couldn't. She wanted to forget the entire thing forever.

When Veronica returned to the Inn, a message was waiting for her at the front desk. It was from her boss, Mark.

Great, now he's haunting me in Tarrytown, like there aren't enough ghosts following me around right now.

She had decided to shower first before calling Mark. She needed the time to chill out from the bizarre experience she had at her Uncle's house, besides Mark could wait. She was sure he was going to lecture her anyway.

After delaying the inevitable, as long as possible she took a deep breath, then dialed the phone.

"Hi, Mark what's on your mind?"

"Where were you last night? I called you three times leaving three messages."

"I didn't know I had to check in with you every five minutes, besides I spent the night at my Uncle's old place. I never got your messages."

"I didn't know you still had a living relative."

"I don't, the house was my inheritance."

"Well, that's all wonderful, but you should have called the Inn. Look, our reputation is on the line here, so listen up."

"I was exhausted when I arrived and the time just got away from me. But I promise to *shape up or ship out, sir.*"

"Loose the sarcasm, will you?"

"In any case, it's a little insulting for you to reiterate journalism 101 to me."

"Since you've forgotten how to report properly, I needed to remind you. I don't want any 'ambush journalism' that seems to be your forte' lately. Leave out the aggressive tactics and the harsh news commentary, and for Pete sakes, leave out your own opinion, just report the facts."

"Well, sometimes that's the way I feel about a situation and I want my viewers to know that."

"Veronica, first off, you're not on an opinion show, and secondly, I'm telling you that this is your final warning. If you don't report according to standards, I will have to fire you." Mark shouted into the phone, as if he was talking to one of his sons.

"All right, but that's the new wave of Journalism today, so don't worry about it so much."

Mark shouted into the telephone, causing Veronica to move the receiver away from her ear. "Well that's not the way we do things at this news station, and it never will be. I have a stellar reputation and I'm not going to let some hard-headed know-it-all ruin that!"

"Okay, okay. I'll be a good little reporter. Even though I think you're wrong," she muttered under her breath.

"What did you say?"

"Nothing, just clearing my throat."

Mark counted to ten in order to calm down and continued, "I've set up some contacts for you that I'd like you to meet today."

"What contacts?"

"First off, you need to go to the Tarrytown Sheriff's office and talk with Sergeant Bishop, who arrested the mother, and get his take on things, and also review his files, and then you need to talk to Mrs. Catherine French with Child Welfare Services, who runs the organization where the baby was left by his mother."

"Am I allowed to follow my own leads, or is this a puppet show to make you look good, and quench the fire of the other news stations?"

"Veronica, do it the way I say. If you come up with anything, another lead...whatever, run it by me first. Got it?"

"Yes, I got it."

"Call me after you speak to these two people."

"All right, don't get all bent out of shape."

"I mean it, Veronica. Don't force me to fire you."

"I won't. I promise."

"Good, talk to you tomorrow then."
"Yeah, talk to you tomorrow."

Veronica hung up the phone, slid onto the sofa, then buried her face in a throw pillow. She felt like a wounded puppy. Suddenly she wasn't at the top of her game anymore. Suddenly she felt small, unimportant and lost, just liked she had every time her mother went into a manic rage.

CHAPTER SEVEN

Veronica walked up to the entrance of the police station. She took inventory of the building. "Hmm, I wonder if this place doubles as a school, or maybe a church, it's really primitive."

She opened the door and approached the reception area. "May I help you?" The young police officer at the reception desk looked up from her paperwork.

"Yes, I'm Veronica Wheaton from Heritage World News. I have an appointment with Sergeant Bishop." Veronica extended her hand in a handshake.

"Yes Ms. Wheaton, he's expecting you." The young police officer withdrew her hand.

She got up from her chair and walked to an office on the right-hand side of the long hallway; the police officer came back a minute later.

"Please have a seat. Sergeant Bishop will be with you shortly."

Veronica acknowledged with a nod, and made her way to an empty chair by the doorway. She scanned the area, assessing the caliber of the police department.

Small town cops, that's for sure. Only two chairs in the waiting room for visitors, no coffee machine, no magazines, and Police Officers that look like they've been transported from Mayberry R.F.D.

Sergeant Bishop came out of his office and meandered down the hallway toward her. Veronica was drawn to his muscular physique; jet black wavy hair and large black olive eyes.

As he approached, Veronica prepared herself by getting mentally into investigative mode. The last thing she needed was to act like a school girl around this country bumpkin of a detective, no matter how gorgeous he appeared to be. Yet something about him was familiar.

"Hello, Ms. Wheaton. Please come into my office."

"Thank you Sergeant Bishop. Your name rings a bell with me for some reason." Veronica wrinkled her nose.

"I've lived in Tarrytown all my life, up on Hillside Circle." The sergeant's smile was warm and inviting.

Then it hit her. It was Brent Bishop, that gigolo from high school. "How are you, Brent?" She gave an insincere smile.

"Veronica Wheaton! They told me a reporter from Heritage World News, named Ms. Wheaton was coming, but they didn't tell me you were Veronica Wheaton. You're looking good, back then you were a mousy looking kid."

"I see you're the same egomaniac," Veronica stared down at him.

"I'm sorry, that came out wrong. I meant, you've turned into a beautiful woman, and talented too from what I hear."

"Nice save, Sergeant," Veronica grinned.

Brent Bishop's desk looked like it had been run over by a bus, papers and files were tossed in every direction. *How does he get anything done?* He sifted through a few piles, then pulled out a folder and handed it to her.

"As you can see, the Martin case was quite a complex one."

"How can you tell with all the well-organized information you have there on that desk?" Veronica stared at him.

Brent Bishop furrowed his brow. "I can assure you that my staff is top–notch, the best police force in Westchester."

"I'm sure." Veronica's tone of voice ridiculed him. Brent glanced through the file ignoring her remark.

"Michelle Martin, the twenty-year-old mother of Ryan Martin, a new-born, no more than a few weeks old, at the time of his abandonment, was declared mentally incompetent during the competency hearing." Sergeant Bishop rattled off as if giving a news conference.

"Why a competency hearing if she left the kid? I thought you could leave babies at precincts, churches, hospitals…" Veronica waved her hand in dismissal.

"Yes, you can, but the note said she was being chased by her husband, who beat her, and now she has resurfaced wanting the kid back."

"And…" Veronica gave Brent her famous eye stare that could chill a person to the bone, but he remained focused.

"Now it becomes an investigation, not just a simple drop-off. When Michelle Martin was examined by a doctor, it had been established that the wounds were self-inflicted," he glared back at her."

"Oh, and so who got the doctor, the court… the husband? And what of the first hospital examination that said the wounds weren't self-inflicted?" She glanced down at her file. "I also see here that her husband was on the city council. Using a few connections, perhaps, to cover up his weakness, shall we say?"

"First off, the first medical report was only an assessment from a medical intern in the emergency room, and secondly, we checked that angle of a cover-up by the husband. Perhaps you didn't notice that in the report it states he had been cleared of charges in his court hearing."

"Of course, he had been cleared," she rolled her eyes.

"Look that's the law. Without enough evidence…well." Sergeant Bishop's voice was strained.

"I know, I know, but what about his treatment of her?"

"That's only her word against his." His eyes narrowed.

"Yes I know, it's *he said, she said*! You're skimming over the emotional abuse for one thing. It can lead a person to do things that they normally wouldn't. It can brainwash a person."

"What proof do we have of emotional abuse? Even if we had some, that still solves nothing in this case, because there is no hard evidence, not to mention that the hospital said she was unstable." Brent lowered his voice in deliberate tones.

"Of course she was unstable; she just gave away her baby! And to answer your question, it can solve everything, if you would only open up to the possibility, and as for evidence; perhaps an expert who has had no connection to Mr. Martin's past career on city council would be a better choice, don't you think?" her tone of voice mocked him.

"Look, Ms. Wheaton, what's your aim here? To take down my department, or find the truth?" He got up from his desk.

"My aim is to get to the truth," she stared back at him.

"And somehow you think our P.D. and the court systems were negligent or, worse, involved in a cover-up?" Brent's nostrils flared as he spoke.

"No, Brent, what I'm saying is that emotional abuse can lead a person to desperate acts that seem inconceivable to the ordinary person. No physical wounds, no crime had been committed, except against that woman's sensibilities."

"We have early records from before her marriage stating that she was hospitalized." Brent handed Veronica a folder.

"So this proves nothing. Haven't you ever heard that abuse is a cycle; she may have been emotionally abused by a parent, or relative. Besides, according to this report, she was hospitalized one year before her wedding, no prior problems, and to my knowledge, she had known Mr. Martin then."

"Yes, she had, but that doesn't prove that her problems started with him. And by the way, we checked out that scenario, and the fact is there hadn't been any signs of physical abuse evident by the husband before, or after the marriage."

"And where is he now?"

Brent sat down. "We aren't sure, he's no longer in Tarrytown and we haven't been able to locate him."

"How convenient," she smirked.

"The law says innocent until proven guilty," Brent's voice rose a pitch.

"Yeah, I know. I would like the address of the hospital where Michelle is in residence."

"Fine, but you're beating a dead horse."

"Well, let me make my own determination. That's what I'm here for isn't it?"

Brent wrote the information on a piece of paper and handed it to Veronica. "Here, be my guest," he huffed.

Veronica got up from the chair and extended her hand for a handshake. "It was *almost* nice seeing you again, Brent."

"Veronica, I'm not who I used to be," Brent said, his expression that of a wounded puppy.

"So, I should care, why?"

"Veronica, let's call a truce. We'll be working on this together for a while, and that's why you should care."

"I work solo," she glared at him.

"I can't have you snooping around without my knowledge."

"Listen, I work solo. I'll keep you updated," she huffed.

"As long as you know your place; no interfering without my consent, agreed?"

Veronica shook her head in a half-hearted yes.

"Look, it's lunchtime, how about we have a bite together for old time's sake, and because it would be a bad rap for me if you walked out of here in a huff." He blew out a breath.

"I'd rather not."

"You have to eat, don't you?"

"Well, alright, but just this once."

"There's a nice diner across the street; they make great burgers," Brent said, as he opened the door for Veronica. She gave him a look of derision as she walked out the door.

They ordered burgers and fries. As they waited for the food, Veronica used it as an opportunity to grill him about his personal life.

"So are you married?

"No, was once."

"I guess she got tired of your flirting with all the young police officers," Veronica smirked.

Brent's eyes glared back at her. "She died three years ago from cancer."

"Oh, I'm sorry."

"I truly loved her," Brent stared out the window.

"How about you, ever marry?"

"Nope, my work is my husband."

"How sad for you."

"I'm not a charity case. I like it that way," Veronica's eyes pierced through him.

"I wasn't suggesting that. I just meant life can be pretty lonely when you haven't anyone.

"I don't find it that way." she shrugged.

As Veronica ate her burger, she wondered what cruel fate had brought her to Tarrytown, and back into Brent Bishop's life. Her mother had always said she'd haunt her from her grave. Veronica was sure she had conjured this thing up, from wherever she was in the hereafter, as payback.

CHAPTER EIGHT

As Veronica stood on the front porch of the large Victorian home, waiting for someone to answer the doorbell, she noticed three children looking at her through the large picture window of what appeared to be a parlor. Their clothes were tattered and worn and their faces were dirty.

For a split second, Veronica considered doing a piece on the care of the kids in this institution, but then she heard Mark's words ringing in her head, and decided to stick with the program.

"Hello, may I help you?" An elderly woman with silver–blue hair and pleasant voice opened the door.

"I'm Veronica Wheaton, reporter for Heritage World News. I have an appointment with Mrs. Catherine French."

"I'm Catherine French," she smiled as she extended a hand.

"Do you run this place?"

"Yes, I do. Please come in." Mrs. French led the way. Veronica took mental notes as to the condition of the place while she walked through the long corridor, that led to a tiny parlor that doubled as a library, at the back of the house. To her surprise, everything seemed clean and bright. Children were laughing and playing in the courtyard, their clothes clean and their hair neatly groomed.

Perhaps I made a rash judgment; maybe the kids I saw had just gotten dirty while playing in the courtyard.

"Have a seat, Ms. Wheaton. What can I do for you?"

Veronica took a small recorder out of her purse and placed it

on the table. "Well, I'd like to record our conversation, if I may."
Veronica stared at Mrs. French sending the message that she really
didn't have an option, but the woman seemed unaffected.

"Why of course, we have nothing to hide here at the Children's
Haven."

"Great, then let's begin. What do you remember about the
morning you found baby Ryan Martin at your doorstep?"

"I recall that we had just gotten the children on the bus for school.
Just as my staff and I began our weekly meeting, our maintenance
man came rushing into my office. He asked me to step outside with
him for a moment, telling me he found a baby on the back steps,
and that he had brought it to the infirmary."

Veronica leaned forward in her chair. "You mean outside to the
baby?"

Mrs. French shook her head. "No, no...outside of my office."

"Oh, and then what happen?" Veronica's eyes narrowed.

"Ms. Wheaton, we find children at our doorstep all the time.
This is a home run by the state and we must follow procedure. What
Mr. Wilkes did was to follow protocol."

"Fine, so what happened next?" Veronica waved her hand in
dismissal.

"After I released my staff—"

"You mean you went back to your meeting?" Veronica's voice
rose an octave.

"Of course not! I meant I went back into the meeting and
dismissed them." Her forehead vein bulged.

"I'm sorry, I misunderstood." Veronica smirked.

"I know what you trying to do, Ms. Wheaton, and it won't work.
This home has a very fine reputation and it has for many years."

"Okay, okay, then what happened next?"

"Mr. Wilkes went back to work landscaping the grounds and I
went into the infirmary, where our nurse was tending to the baby."

"So did you do an evaluation of his condition?"

"Yes, we did."

"First, Nurse Kinney cleaned him up and put dry clothes on him, while she waited for my arrival, to supervise the examination."

"Did you or your nurse notice any markings on the child?"

"If you're referring to signs of abuse; no, not at all! He appeared very well cared for."

"What do you mean by 'very well cared for', Mrs. French?"

"Well, he had fine baby clothes, you know the kind you get from a fancy boutique. The mother had taken good care of him at the time he was left on the doorstep, putting a fresh pair of clothes, two diapers, a bottle and some toys in with him."

"Is that unusual?" Veronica wrinkled her nose.

"Yes, most of the infants come from young unwed mothers, who haven't any financial resources to purchase such items."

"I was told there was a note pinned to him. Can you tell me about that?"

"Yes, there was, and it was given to the police."

"What did the note say?"

"Please take care of Ryan. He is a good boy and very loving. They are out to get me and I must go. He's coming. I can't wait or he'll kill me."

"Hmm, first it's they, then it's him! What do you make of that?"

"Well, she is clearly psychotic. If she was referring to only her husband, she would not have said 'they'."

"On the other hand, it's entirely possible that her husband was involved with someone else, or a group who wanted her dead, the mafia, a drug smuggling ring; maybe she saw something."

"I suppose that's possible, but the police said the mother had a history of mental illness. Besides the husband was a banker at the time, and in the past, had served on the city council."

"That doesn't make him an upstanding citizen; maybe he had a night job."

"I suppose that's possible, but that's all I know about the case."

"Where is baby Ryan now?"

"He's living with a foster family and doing quite well."

"Where are they?"

"I'm not at liberty to divulge that information."

"Oh, I see."

"Ms. Wheaton, where the child is living is immaterial to your investigation. If you have further questions, please talk with Sergeant Bishop."

Mrs. French got up from her seat to indicate the interview was over.

"Well, that's where you're wrong, it is important to my investigation, and thanks, I will take it up with the Sergeant."

Veronica sensed that the woman was telling the truth. She could not find any reason to believe the home was negligent, or that Mrs. French was lying about the situation. The entire episode of Baby Ryan's abandonment perplexed her. There had to be a loophole, and yet, there was none – at least not here.

The sun was setting over the Hudson River, leaving golden beams of light on the water. She stood at the river's edge breathing in the air, reluctant to return to her room, but duty called.

Veronica took one last deep breath of the fresh air, and then retired to her hotel room. Then she called Mark with the details of her interviews. After their conversation, she went straight to bed.

Now scenes of her days romanticizing about Brent played out in her head. She recalled having come home after the initial rejection by Brent. It had been prom season, and her friend, Meg, had a date and had begged Veronica to accept her boyfriend's cousin's invite. Veronica had taken one look at the skinny geek with thick glasses and passed on the invitation.

As Veronica sat in her room that prom night reading a book, and holding back her tears, her uncle and Mom entered the room.

"So what's this about turning down Meg's cousin?" Uncle Jeb asked.

"I just don't want to go; besides, men can't be trusted." Veronica huffed.

"Well, I can certainly understand that—" Uncle Jeb's reassurance was broken by the squeal of her mother.

"You're an idiot, don't you know that's not normal. She needs therapy," Mom shouted at him, her eyes all aflame.

"But she's just upset." Uncle Jeb choked out the word, as if he was afraid to talk.

"She's not normal. I was afraid this would happen. God couldn't be satisfied with screwing me up; He had to screw her up too!"

On that note, Veronica's mother and uncle had exited the room. Uncle Jeb turned back and gave Veronica a compassionate glance, while her mother had slammed the door so hard behind her, it had made the stuffed animals on the bookshelf tumble to the ground. As she picked up the stuffed toys, the stinging words of her mother rang through her head. *She's not normal, God screwed her up.*

CHAPTER NINE

The next morning Veronica felt like she'd been run over by a truck. Her body ached, her head pounded, and she felt herself unraveling bit by bit. She had cried last night in a way she hadn't shed tears since childhood, and what was most alarming to her, was the fact that she could not stop the flood of tears that fell onto her pillow.

Today she needed to visit Michelle Martin at the county psychiatric hospital before she attempted locating the father. Veronica was reluctant to meet her, because of the mental ward situation; it felt too much like living her childhood over again.

Enough dwelling on the past, I can handle anything, Veronica told herself. She shook off the ominous mood, and then headed for the bathtub. The hot, steamy water that she filled with the hotel's complimentary lavender beads, had proven to have a calming effect, giving her the edge she needed to tackle the Michelle Martin situation.

Veronica dressed in her blue jeans and white blouse, pulling her long black hair back into a ponytail. She wanted to make Michelle Martin feel comfortable, by looking like an ordinary everyday woman, and not a reporter in pursuit of a hot scoop.

As she sped down the highway, she wondered how anyone could allow themselves to get in such a condition. Sure, some people had real mental issues, but Michele Martin merely had a breakdown shortly after she met her husband, Robert. Two scenarios could play out here, one being it was probably new relationship jitters; or more likely an abusive husband.

As far as the note pinned to the baby; that needed to be pursued. In her opinion, the local police hadn't shown clear evidence that Michelle had pinned the note on the baby, or, for that fact, even left the baby at the doorstep. When questioned, Brent said she was not responsive and the doctor claimed she was traumatized by the entire situation.

"Hmm, if she was so traumatized as they say, then maybe she was forced into giving her child up?" Veronica scratched her head, it was something worth considering.

Robert had the perfect defense in convincing the experts his wife was unstable, even to the point of attempting suicide. "What a great solution, he's free, the baby is in a good place and he, being the loving father, wants his child to have a family, and selflessly gives baby Ryan up for adoption. What a Lifetime movie special this would make!"

Veronica approached the main reception, and took a deep breath. Something about the place unnerved her, but she couldn't quite figure out what was making her so apprehensive.

"Yes, may I help you?" The middle-aged volunteer in a white hospital coat asked.

"I'm Veronica Wheaton, reporter for Heritage World News. I have an interview with Michelle Martin," Veronica showed her credentials.

The woman carefully checked her credentials, and then ushered her to the waiting area. "Have a seat and I'll let them know you're here."

Veronica nodded in agreement, then took a seat next to the magazine rack. She scanned the selection; *Psychology Today, Mental Health*; she turned away in disgust. *Why would anybody want to read about mental illness when they are in a mental ward?*

A tall, slender young woman, wearing a lab coat, came out of a doorway from the left corridor, she approached Veronica. "Hello, I'm Dr. Amy McDermott, head psychologist for this department."

"Hello, it's a pleasure to meet you."

"I'll take you to the common room where Michelle is waiting."

Veronica sized up the doctor. She looked like she just graduated high school, with her big brown eyes, freckled face and blonde hair. How did she manage to be the head of the department at such a young age? *Maybe there was a juicy story there she could work on? Well, I best not borrow anymore trouble with Mark right now.*

They walked down the hallway to a large sitting room, as they made their way down the hallway, Veronica studied everything, from the color of the walls, to the patients in the hallways. Something seemed so familiar to her. Veronica's mother had been in a place somewhere in Tarrytown when she was young, but she was sure the name of the place was different.

The Doctor opened the wooden double doors and approached Michelle, who was sitting in the corner, biting her fingernails. "Michelle this is Ms. Wheaton."

"Hu... Hello." The young, frail girl averted eye contact with Veronica, still chewing on her fingernail, in a nervous and fidgety way. She acted as if she was afraid of her *or maybe afraid of something she dare not speak of?*

"Hello, I'm happy to meet you." Veronica smiled and extended a hearty handshake, and the young girl relaxed a little bit.

"I'll be right here." The doctor pointed to a chair next to the sofa."

"Ah, I'd prefer if you stayed in the distance, or in the hall, that would be even better," Veronica pointed to the door.

"Please, Ms. Wheaton, I'll need to monitor her behavior. This may upset her."

"I'll only move to that corner over there." The doctor pointed to a seat by a window, directly across from where they were seated.

"Very well then, but don't jump up every time she sighs, will you?" Veronica shot her a cold stare.

Dr. McDermott gave Veronica a look of disapproval, then moved to the designated area.

"So Michelle, are you comfortable? Maybe you'd like a soda?" Veronica smiled.

"No, no, I'm fine," Michelle said while staring at the floor.

Veronica moved closer to her, and spoke in a soft voice, "I'm not going to bite you, Michelle. You can relax and if anything makes you uncomfortable, just tell me, okay?"

"Sure, okay," Michelle's expression softened and Veronica started the interview.

"So Michelle, tell me about yourself, where did you grow up?"

"In Maryland until we moved to New Jersey."

"So, you and your parents moved away?"

"Yeah, I was twelve."

"Why did you move?"

"Dad got a new job." She took a thoughtful pause and continued. "It seems he always changed jobs."

"Why is that?"

"He drank a lot."

"So, he went to work drunk, then—"

"Yeah, then he got fired."

"Did he ever hit you?"

"Only once, nothing bad, but I answered him back." Michelle turned away and gazed out of the window. The doctor started toward her, but Veronica motioned for her to stay put, giving her that famous sapphire eye stare.

"I see, so how did you meet your husband?"

"He worked for Dad at the auto shop?"

"Your dad owned an auto shop?"

"Yeah, in New Jersey."

"So, your father must have worked hard somehow to be able to buy that place."

"Yeah, well, Mom saved as much of his salary from the different jobs he had as she could. When the guy who owned it retired, Dad bought it from him with the down payment from Mom's money."

"That must have made your mother upset."

"No, not really. She figured he finally was doing something constructive with his life."

"Does he still own it?"

"No, he died three years ago."

"I was under the impression that your husband was on the city council or something like that, and that he also worked for a bank."

"Oh, he was, at one time on city council. He was always bucking heads with someone. He only worked for a bank a few months before we split."

"What happened?"

Michelle got a bit nervous, biting off one of her fingernails. The doctor stood up and was about to approach Michelle when she began to answer the question.

"He was accused of taking a bribe, but he was acquitted. It was some girl in the office who had it out for him for some reason."

"Oh, I see." Veronica squeezed Michelle's arm to reassure her, then continued to ask, "What happened to your mom?"

"She died when I was seventeen."

"Oh, I'm sorry." Veronica gave a warm smile and continued, "so, back to the shop; is it still in operation?"

"Robert inherited it, but it's not currently operating."

"Why did Robert inherit it and not you?"

"Robert convinced Dad he could run it on my behalf."

"Oh, I see, and you said nothing about it?"

"I was afraid of them."

"You said afraid of them, you were afraid of your father too?"

"Yes, he had a temper."

"Did he ever hurt you? You mentioned he hit you once, but was it more than that, Michelle?"

Now Dr. McDermott stood in place, and in a stern voice say, "Ms. Wheaton, may I remind you—"

Before she could finish Veronica put her hand up in a motion to silence her.

"Okay, back to the business. Was it a thriving business?"

"I suppose. Dad had plenty of people going in and out."

"For auto repairs?"

"Some of his customers didn't even have cars. He said they were consulting about work." Michelle diverted her glace.

"What work?"

"I assume mechanics," she shrugged.

"Did Robert have the same clients?"

"Yeah"

"So tell me about you and Robert."

At this point Michelle stiffened up and Veronica re-directed.

"I'm thirsty. I'm going to get a soda. Do you want one?"

"No, no thanks."

Veronica went to the machine in the back of the room where Dr. McDermott was seated. "I think she's had enough for one day, Ms. Wheaton." The doctor stated in a low tone of voice.

"Just give me five more minutes, will you?" Veronica glared at her and the Doctor backed down. Veronica turned on her heals and headed back to Michelle.

"So where were we? Oh yes, you and Robert."

"We were happy; he treated me well, and he always bought me nice things."

"So he was happy about the baby?"

"Well, no. Things changed after he found out. He didn't want kids, but I wanted the baby. I couldn't get rid of it." Michelle touched her stomach.

"Did he want you to abort it?"

"Yes, he did."

"Robert started yelling all the time; sometimes he'd slap me, once I fell and he thought I lost the baby."

"Was he upset when you didn't?"

"Yes, that's when—" Michelle started to tremble.

"That's when what—, Michelle?"

"I don't want to talk anymore."

She started to sniffle and the doctor came over, placing her hand on Michelle's shoulder, "I think you should leave now, Ms. Wheaton. Michelle's had enough for one day."

"I'm not here to hurt her," Veronica glared at Dr. McDermott.

"Well, that's debatable," the doctor huffed.

"Listen, Doctor, you have your job and I have mine."

"Please go," Dr. McDermott said, as she pointed toward the door.

"I'd like to try again tomorrow. I only need ten more minutes."

"We'll see!"

The doctor tried to block her view of Michelle, but Veronica peeked over her shoulder. "Michelle, can I come tomorrow to visit?" she said, giving the doctor a glaring look.

"I suppose so."

"See, Doctor, Michelle said yes," she smirked.

Veronica's piercing sapphire eyes caused the doctor to tremble. Veronica walked away, pleased to have won the battle.

Veronica drove off, satisfied with the interview so far. But her soul was unsettled, she seemed to be having an out of body experience, as she again, found herself at Hillcrest Manor. Bewildered, she exited the car, and walked to the courtyard that faced the Hudson River. She stood facing the river for several minutes, allowing the wind to cover her face. Then something her rational mind could not comprehend occurred. As if carried on the throws of the river winds, she heard someone say, "I have loved you with an everlasting love." She looked around, glancing from one side to the other, but no one could be found.

Dazed and bewildered, she walked back to the car and headed for the hotel.

Was she delusional? Maybe she needed to see one of those doctors at… No, no she wasn't going to entertain those kinds of thoughts.

When she got back to the hotel the telephone message light

flashed at her. She played it back bracing herself for Mark's lecture. She hadn't called earlier as promised.

"Hello, Veronica. It's Roy. You've been on my mind today. Hope all is well; did you get a chance to read the book? Take care now. The book! That was where she'd seen those same words she had heard while walking by the river".

Veronica darted to the bedroom nightstand, there glaring at her was the words, "I have loved you with an everlasting love."

She quickly tossed herself on the bed and began to read the book.

Dear Reader,

So you're in a bad place right now and your entire world may be falling down around you. You thought you were in control, but you found out that isn't so.

Be at peace, because there is one that loves you beyond all you could possibly have dreamed of.

John 3:16 says, God so love the world that He gave His only begotten Son so that the world might be saved.

Veronica could not put the book down. She read on into the night. She read about God's plan for salvation, about how Jesus died to take her place of punishment. Suddenly, she felt so small, so broken, like a tiny seashell crushed by the weight of the crashing waves upon the sand.

Could she believe this stuff, was it real?

She was too tired to find out. Memories of another time in her past flooded her dreams. She was with her mother and father at the hospital, Mom had been ill. She recalled the doctors slapping restraints on her mother because she was uncontrollable. Veronica remembered feeling sorry for her Mom, thrashing about trying to free herself. She looked so small and frightened lying on the bed all tied up. She recalled her mom telling the doctor that she was her brave little soldier; that was the first time Veronica actually felt loved by her mother, and it made her proud.

Then it dawned on her the reason the county hospital bothered her—it *was* the place where her mother suffered that fatal breakdown, but back then it was called Mercy Hospital. What was going on? Was this a cruel trick to get her to go nuts, just like her mother? Who would do such a cruel thing? Or was this what Roy called *Divine Providence?*

CHAPTER TEN

The conversation with Michelle Martin baffled Veronica, as her answers were coherent in spite of having been in a psychiatric ward. Veronica believed that she was a by-product of a failed system, just like her mother. At night, illusions from the past swept her rest away. Veronica averted the thought of having her mother's disease. *Contrary to others' opinions, I'm not like my mother!* Those comments stung her to the bone; especially when her sweet Dad, exasperated, uttered them. Today those remarks sustained power over her.

Veronica pondered over how her behavior resembled that of her mother. She didn't have mood swings. At times, she daunted those who dare to cross her, but those were the spoils of unmended wounds. How was she deemed to be unscathed by such an unbearable upbringing?

Veronica decided to research the disease and its effects on family members. The gained knowledge would aid her in conducting a competitive investigation while at the same time, confronting the demons of her past.

She drove to the local library located directly across from her old high school. Scenes from those after school days flooded her mind. Veronica had always known that she wanted to be a journalist, and devoured such books at the library. Now she was back at ground zero, bewildered by the unfolding ordeal. At the reference materials section, she found a few books on mental illnesses. She took them and ambled to an isolated table in the back of the library.

The bipolar disorder symptoms outlined were habitual behavior: *calculated emotional abuse aimed to manipulate the victim.* Things she already knew, such as the person with the disorder needs to control everyone and everything. She always felt her mom did and said things intended to shame her, by imposing control and displaying her superiority. As a result, Veronica became an over–achiever, and she shuttered at the thought. The acknowledgment evoked memories of a conversation she had had with her mom when Brent rebuffed their relationship. *"It's all your fault, Veronica. Besides nobody wants you anyway. You undoubtedly did something wrong."*

How can a child be emotionally healthy, if a child is always shunned, jilted and starved of love of a parent? How can one learn selfhood and acceptance of others, if that virtue is lacking reinforcement at home?

But Veronica did thrive and grow. However, it was not healthy, that she had to admit. Michelle, on the other hand, married and ended up scarred by a series of unfortunate events.

She drove along the Hudson River without purpose, until reaching a small park at the river's edge. The river breeze soothed her thoughts, as she watched the rows of daffodils that dotted its edge, dance to the rhythm of the wind.

What was she to do with this new revelation? In one way, it was freeing to know she wasn't alone in her suffering, but in another way, it only caused her more unwanted pain and memory triggers; things she thought were tucked away for good.

She rested on an old wooden bench and watched the river flow on downstream, crashing against the rocks along the river's edge. Tears rolled down her cheeks. The wind brought whispers of the past. "Baby, it's not your fault." "I know Daddy," she murmured.

The dancing beans of twilight over the Hudson River hushed Veronica back to the car. She pondered where this recent discovery of truth would lead her.

CHAPTER ELEVEN

Veronica woke up with the book Roy had given her tucked between her left cheek, and her pillow. As she stretched out in the bed, she felt something pinching her foot. She pulled a piece of crinkled-up paper from under the sheets, then sat on the edge of the bed, flattening out the paper, and read it. The note had been written by Roy.

Veronica,

> *The meaning of your name is 'true face', and it is not by accident that you've come by this name. You've always sought your interpretation of truth. Now seek His truth, and you will gain His peace.*

Godspeed,
Roy

She wept without restraint, as each sob pulsated deeper within her anguish. For a moment she felt alone and frightened, just like a child longing for love.

She took hold of the book and ran her fingers over the title; "I have loved you with an everlasting love." The words *everlasting love* echoed in her mind. Out of desperation, she fell to her knees, and prayed, "God, I'm not sure about this Jesus thing, it's all so weird, why would you send your son to die for someone who doesn't even know Him?"

At that moment, she remembered the words of the book, "I knew you before you were knit in your mother's womb." She recalled Roy's conversion story. He was a raging alcoholic, angry at the world, hurting his wife and kids. He'd been sober ever since giving his life to Christ, Her investigative nature told her, although he sounded genuine; she needed to verify the facts. She did some research and confirmed his claims; he really had been completely healed. On the other hand, Veronica wasn't ready then to meet the Lord, so she had dismissed it as coincidental.

Veronica re-evaluated her position, after all, what did she has to lose! Down on her knees, she sensed her pride was being stripped away, her dignity shattered, and feeling small and powerless as a newborn baby.

"Jesus, I don't know about you, or your father. What I do know is Roy has always been honest with me and his love for you shows in his dealings with others. If you're indeed, the great healer he claims you are, please take me, and this entire ugly mess of my life, and help me!"

Veronica was overwhelmed by a sense of peace and love, such as she never experienced before.

She clinched to her previous resolution of doing everything in her power to help Michelle Martin get back on her feet, to find her husband, and to dig out the hidden truth. Maybe by helping this young girl, she could somehow make up for what lacked in their relationship with her mother. This would be her first step to redeeming the past, facing the future, and starting a new life.

After careful consideration, Veronica concluded that her bitterness was rooted in her inability to dismay the concealed poison of the past, that control her reckless life! *Isn't it funny how I never recognized that before, perhaps this Jesus thing is real. Quoting Roy: "Only time will tell?"*

CHAPTER TWELVE

Veronica took a deep breath, then approached the front desk of the psych ward.

"Hello, my name is Veronica Wheaton, reporter for Heritage World News, Rhode Island. I was here yesterday to see—"

"Yes, I remember you," interrupted the irked young nurse.

"I just need to talk with Ms. Martin again," pleaded Veronica. She struggled to keep her non–confrontational attitude, and hoped that her newly discovered God given strength and serenity were real, as assured in the book. She was amazed at the uplifting power of one short prayer. She felt as if a big burden has been removed from her shoulders, just as described by Roy, but doubted it. For the first time, she understood, and knew what Roy meant; she was not alone in the struggle.

"Look, Ms. Wheaton, my supervisor gave me specific instructions to keep you away from Ms. Martin."

"May I know why? Yesterday, Ms. Martin agreed to another visit." Veronica's eyes narrowed.

"Because your visit yesterday, upset her, and we had to sedate her."

"Sedate her? When I left she was perfectly fine with my coming today. Albeit, a little upset, but that's to be expected." Veronica looked confused.

The nurse got up from her chair, and leaned over the counter, staring Veronica straight in the eye, "Ms. Wheaton, do I need to call security?"

Veronica felt the heat rush to her cheeks. "Was this embarrassment?" She was not accustomed to feeling that emotion. Once more, she felt sensitive to the response of the desk nurse.

Veronica shook her head,"No, no. I understand. I only wondered why the change. Thank you."

Veronica turned to leave the hospital; her eyes began to fill with tears. *Was she feeling wounded, or sorrow for Michelle?* She didn't know which. It was all so perplexing. She whispered a silent prayer, as she headed for the elevators. "Please God, I'm new at this faith business, help me understand what's happening, because right now I want to pounce all over that that...woman, but by the same token, I know she's only doing her job. Hmm, when did I ever care about that."

As Veronica waited for the elevator, she heard a commotion coming from the right side of the corridor. She turned to see two aides trying to keep Michelle Martin from bolting from their grasp.

"Let me go. I don't want meds!" Then she spotted Veronica. "Ms. Wheaton, please help me!" She screamed as tears freely ran down her cheeks.

Veronica went to her side. "It's okay Michelle, I'm here." Veronica gave the unfeeling aides a cold stare as she spoke, "Will one of you go find Dr. McDermott, pronto!"

The young aides were afraid of Veronica, at that point both left Michelle standing alone with her.

"I've got to get out of here now!" Michelle shouted, as she tried to bolt from Veronica's hold.

"Michelle, please calm down. This behavior isn't going to help you at all."

"Well, if you got locked away because your husband's—." Michelle thought better of finishing the sentence.

"Your husband is what, Michelle?" Veronica looked her in the eye, but the young girl froze in place, realizing she had almost spilled the truth.

"Nothing, you're right, I need to calm down."Michelle nodded her head in a gesture of agreement, hands at her side; head down, like a wounded puppy.

Just then, Dr. McDermott walked into the room. Her shoulders pinched back, her walk purposeful with each step, and with an angry expression that could make a mighty lion cower down.

"Is there a problem here, Ms. Wheaton?" she snarled.

"Well, there seems to be; Ms. Martin expressed an interest in leaving this facility."

"Oh, I see, so you're now an expert on psychological disorders." Her tone was sarcastic at best.

"Can we go somewhere and talk?" Veronica took a deep breath to keep her cool.

"Certainly," the doctor said, looking half amused and half annoyed.

"Gentlemen, take Ms. Martin back to her room and keep guard over her."

Veronica motioned for them to halt. "I believe Ms. Martin should be in the meeting. It's her life we're talking about." Veronica's resolve was firm, even though she was shaking on the inside; she seemed to be outside herself, as if something, or someone else was at the reins.

"Very well then, Ms. Martin, come with me," the doctor smirked.

They entered Dr. McDermott's office, and she motioned for them to take a seat.

"So, Ms. Wheaton, enlighten me with your medical knowledge, will you?"

"Look, Dr. McDermott, I'm not trying to overstep your authority or anything of that sort."

"Oh, really; you could have fooled me," she annunciated each word for dramatic effect.

Michelle began to fidget, and Veronica reached for her hand, taking it in hers for moral support.

Veronica took a deep breath before she spoke, "As I was saying,

I was on my way out, when Michelle called to me to help her. Don't you find that odd?"

"Not really, patients often try sympathy tactics to gain someone's trust. It's part of their psychosis," she explained.

"Doctor, I find her quite coherent and alert. What I do find, is an entire staff that is focused on keeping this woman in chains." Veronica's sapphire eyes pierced through her stare, as she said a silent prayer that she would keep her cool.

"Oh really now, what makes you an expert."

"You have her listed as bipolar, but you haven't assessed her family history as to any other factors, have you?"

"Her symptoms are classic."

"Doctor McDermott, I was raised by a bipolar mother. I know what it looks, smells, tastes, and sounds like, and this isn't it!" Veronica's nostrils flared, and she told herself she needed to maintain her cool, or she would end up losing this battle.

"I think I've heard enough. You can leave now!" The doctor rose from her desk. When Michelle saw Veronica get out of her chair, she ran to the door to block it.

"Please, don't leave, Ms. Wheaton. Please!"

Veronica turned to the doctor saying, "Do patients who are out of control normally plead for help in such a calm, soft tone of voice?" The doctor didn't respond, but only huffed.

"She can only be released to a family member, and she has no other relatives, except a husband, who cannot be located."

"Yes, but if the person is competent, then she can release herself."

"But, she is not."

"That's your opinion. I want to get an independent assessment of Ms. Martin's condition."

"Very well then, I'll call—"

Veronica interrupted, "I will have my boss call an independent expert. Believe me, he will tend to agree with you, so I can assure you it will be fair."

Veronica turned to Michelle. "Hang in there a little bit longer, okay? Do what they say for now, and we'll get you out of here as soon as possible."

"Okay, Ms. Wheaton, but make it soon."

Veronica hugged her, and then turned toward the doctor. "I'll be in touch."

The doctor didn't utter a word, as Veronica walked out of the office.

The next few days, Veronica worked day and night to get the proper assessment done. She reached out to all her colleagues, but her efforts were in vain. Her boss was less than happy with her interference beyond a news story. However, when Veronica explained her motivation was exclusively Michelle's welfare, and not a juicy story, he changed his mind. Veronica's demeanor was somehow different, and trusting his instinct, he agreed to help.

In the meantime, she prayed and supported Michelle as much as time allowed. She read the Bible that was provided by the hotel, and re-read parts of the book Roy had given her.

She was having an internal struggle: parts of her old self were still with her, and others had disappeared. It was a curious and frightening thing, but Roy assured her that *being a new creation in Christ Jesus* was not an overnight thing.

So, Veronica prayed, and wept, and held onto every word Roy said, as he became her confidante and mentor.

CHAPTER THIRTEEN

Veronica was losing hope that she would ever find someone to help Michelle. Mark called all of his contacts to no avail and she had asked some of her colleagues in the business, but she hadn't any response. She let out a sigh, "How am I going to tell Michelle?" She dressed, got in her car, and headed down the road to see Michelle, wondering all the way there, what to say to her.

She tried to smile as she entered the visiting room, but Michelle saw right through it.

"Wha, what's happened?"

"Nothing...nothing at all, that's the problem?" Veronica threw her hands up in exasperation.

"You mean, about the medical assessment?"

"Yes, the medical assessment!" Veronica snapped.

Michelle cowered down, as if she was a wounded puppy. The nurse got up from her seat in the corner of the room, but Veronica motioned for her to stay put. Then she softened her voice, and continued, "I'm sorry, Michelle. It's just that at times people are so cold and indifferent to the needs of others. But if it were their daughter, or wife, they'd want help."

Michelle's soulful eyes glanced at Veronica's wounded expression.

"Why does this mean so much to you?"

"Why? Because it's not right what's happened to you, and besides this kind of thing could happen to anybody," Veronica huffed.

Michelle peered into Veronica's eyes, and with a compassionate tone sought more information. "There's more you're not telling me, isn't there?"

Veronica let out a big sigh, "Yes, there is."

"So, tell me then."

"Well, my mom was bipolar. I suffered terribly as a child because of her condition."

"How so?"

"She was abusive, emotionally, and then she abandoned me, or at least I thought so all these years." Veronica wiped a tear from her eye.

"What do you mean?" Michelle's eyes widened.

"Well, she got really sick when I was about eight years old. I was sent to live with my Uncle Jeb, here in Tarrytown."

"And you hadn't been back since, right?"

Veronica took a deep breath, and then continued, "Anyway, it really ruined my life. I felt unwanted, ugly, and unlovable."

"Where was your dad in all this?"

"He had been there, with Mom. He was sane—at least I thought he was." And that's the problem.

"So, actually, both of them left you with Uncle Jeb."

"Yes, but I didn't realize that until I got saved."

"You mean the Jesus thing?" Michelle's eyes narrowed.

"Yeah, the Jesus thing. Oh sorry, Michelle, I forgot we haven't talked about this. Before coming here to investigate your case, Roy, a Christian, and co-worker of mine, gave me a book titled, *I Have Loved You with an Everlasting Love*. The book helped me to understand my past, and how Jesus truly loved me. After doing some soul-searching, I started to feel His transforming effect in me, and the way I conducted myself toward others. That is known among Christians as 'being saved.'"

"Ah the Jesus thing!" Michelle nodded.

"You see, I was told my father was gone, and nowhere to be found. Then about a year later, my uncle told me he got word that my dad was killed while driving a pickup truck, somewhere in the Midwest. The realization of his abandonment devastated me. How could he do that to me? The news of his death erased any hope of him coming back to take me home.

Later on, my mom got better, and she came to live with Uncle Jeb and me. It made me so mad, I had to live with her again, and that there wasn't any chance of going to live with my dad."

"But, you still had your Uncle Jeb, and from what you said about him, he was a loving, kind man."

"What do you mean? I just said Mom came back." Veronica narrow her eyes.

Dr. McDermott got up from her seat. "Ms. Wheaton, I don't see how this is beneficial to Ms. Martin."

Veronica blushed. "You're right, I'm sorry."

Michelle stood to face Dr. McDermott. "It's okay, I want to hear this, and it *is* helpful." The doctor nodded and sat down again.

Michelle continued. "I only meant that you said your mom abandoned you, but she did come back, however unstable she had been. Based on what you told me, it seems that your father really had been the one who made the decision to leave you behind, not your mother." Michelle got up, and gave her a warm embrace.

Veronica's tears fell with ease now. She wiped the tears from her eyes, and took several deep breaths to calm herself down. Noticing her distress, Michelle got up and walked to the water cooler and poured a glass of water. While she was at the water cooler, the nurse approached Veronica. She whispered, "I don't think this conversation is helping Michelle, Ms. Wheaton." Veronica nodded in agreement, and then Michelle came back with the water.

"Thanks." Veronica sipped the water, and then said, "We can finish this story another time."

"Oh no, I want to hear it!" Michelle's squeezed her arm.

Veronica looked at the nurse for approval, and she nodded in agreement.

Veronica took a deep breath and continued. "Roy suggested that I look further into the reasons why Dad left. Maybe he had problems of his own and was trying to protect me. Maybe he's still alive; anything is possible."

"But I thought you said your father was killed."

"I had never truly believed that, but I had no way to prove Uncle Jeb wrong. I had to accept it, and move on with my life. However, I had always harbored a notion that Uncle Jeb had been hiding something."

"Where's your uncle and mom now?"

"They both died within a year of each other, a few years back."

"Oh, I'm sorry."

"I didn't go to the funeral; I just couldn't face it, but was told by Uncle Jeb's lawyer that I inherited the house. I told the lawyer to quickly close up Hillcrest Manor, because I couldn't deal with it at the time. In truth, I hadn't wanted nothing to do with it. On the other hand, I wasn't in any frame of mind to sell it either."

"Too much pain for you, huh?"

"Yes, way too much," Veronica sighed.

"But, what about this Jesus thing? If you're as changed as you say, then it shouldn't bother you?"

"Here is the thing about being saved; it doesn't happen in a wave of a wand. True change is a process."

"Well, that's not how the preachers make it sound," Michelle smirked.

"I know, they are only trying to entice people to their church. I found that out a long time ago. That's why I didn't believe in a loving God, or change either, Michelle. Everything in my life dictated that He was an ogre who wanted to pounce on people. My friend Roy, who I mentioned before, has been a Christian for years, and he's been trying to turn me on to this Jesus thing too."

"What changed your mind?"

"There were two events which had a pivotal effect in my life. First, I was totally and completely desperate. Second, this assignment was a last ditch effort by my boss, to keep me out of trouble."

"What trouble?"

"Trouble in my reporting tactics, that's why I'm not at the station; and the fact that he assumed this case would be cut and dry."

"Meaning you'd find out I was crazier than a bedbug?"

"Yeah, that's about it in a nutshell!" Veronica chuckled.

"So, your friend Roy, what about him?"

"Roy gave me this book," Veronica showed it to Michelle. She turned to the cover and read the title out loud. *I Have Loved You with an Everlasting Love.*

"It might sound a little corny, but as I began to read it, a new kind of warm, and fuzzy feeling got a stronghold on me. Then when everything fell apart with this case, my job etc., I got down on my knees, and prayed one of those *Dear God, if there is a God,* prayers."

"What happened?"

"I felt at peace and loved all at once."

"You don't say."

"I know it sounds crazy, but it's true. Over the past two weeks God has shown me what you just told me about my mom and dad. He's shown me the ugliness I harbored in my heart, and little by little he chipped it away."

"Okay, assuming this is true, why are you helping me?" Michelle's stare penetrated Veronica's soul.

"Because I was so wounded, and in such pain, that in order to protect my fragile inner self, I didn't give my mom a chance to redeem herself. When I was able to free myself, I vowed never to look back."

"So I'm your penance?" Michelle's voice was strained.

"No, no. I didn't mean it that way. I never saw who she was, everything about her was always covered in illness. I never said those two powerful words, "I forgive.""

"I understand your guilty feelings, but I'm not a mission project, Veronica."

"I know that, but look how you've been treated, and misunderstood. Perhaps the so-called "experts" are wrong about you. Don't you want your son to have a chance to really know his mom?"

"Yes, more than anything in the entire world," Michelle sniffled.

"That's my motivation; you have a right to be heard, just like my mom did with me."

"I guess I get it."

"Look, I know you don't believe in Jesus Christ, but just read this book, it will make a big difference, I promise." Veronica handed the book over to Michelle.

"Do you know what the name Veronica means?" Michelle asked her.

"Yes I do" Veronica turned to face her. "It means, *true face.* Isn't that something else?"

"I believe in you, Veronica. This assessment will happen."

The conversation was broken by the ring of her cell phone.

"Hello?"

"Hi, Veronica, it's Roy."

"Hi, Roy, how are you?"

"I'm fine. Listen, I called to tell you I heard you're looking for a medical assessment for Michele Martin."

"Yes, I am; do you have a lead?"

"Yeah, I have a cousin in White Plains who is a doctor, so I gave her a call."

"And what did she say?"

"And she has put me in touch with a colleague of hers, who works in the mental health field. Her name is Dr. Janice Bookman. I'll text all her information to you. She is expecting your call."

"Thanks, Roy you're a Godsend, literally!" Veronica laughed.

"God bless you, honey."

"Thanks so much, Roy."

Veronica hung up the phone, and turned toward Michelle. "We have good news. I have a willing assessor for your mental health exam. I'll make the appointment with the doctor for some time next week, and on my way out, I'll tell Dr. McDermott."

"Everything is falling into place, isn't it?" Michelle's smile filled her face.

"That's how God works when we trust him. Now if I could remember that for myself. Anyway, will you read the book?" Veronica asked.

"I'll promise I'll give it a chance."

"That's all I ask, just give him a chance. You won't regret it."

Veronica said a silent prayer of gratitude to God, for all that was happening in Michelle's life, as well as her own. Veronica stopped to write down the information from Roy's text, then made a visit to the restroom, before walking over to the office of Dr. McDermott.

She knocked on the door. "Come in." The doctor called out.

"Dr. McDermott. I have good news. I was able to find a doctor to do another assessment on Michelle. Her name is Doctor Bookman."

"Yes, I overheard you tell Michelle, and I know of her. She's a good doctor; well respected in the field."

"Good, then I'll make an appointment."

"No, Ms. Wheaton, I'll make the appointment. I'm the case doctor here." Dr. McDermott's eyes narrowed.

"Of course!" Veronica blushed.

"I'll let you know the results." The doctor continued.

"May I be here when it takes place?" Veronica asked in a calm tone of voice.

The doctor let out a heavy sigh. "Very well. I'm sure Michelle would want that, but you'll have to stay outside in the waiting area."

"That's fine, and thank you." Veronica left the office and headed on home.

That night, in spite of all the wonderful changes in Michelle's life, and in her life as well, sleep seemed to evade Veronica. The peace she had known earlier gave way to her fears.

What if she was fired, where would she work? What if Michelle failed the test? What if she discovered something about her family she couldn't handle?

What if, What if, What if...

Dear God,

Will I ever be free? I can't change anything by projecting in the unknown future, and even if I could, how do I know what's the right thing for me. Veronica stared at the stars in the night sky.

CHAPTER FOURTEEN

The night before Michelle's assessment, Veronica tossed and turned, as haunting visions of her past kept parading across her mind's eye, just like a silent movie. The vision changed in a flash to Veronica's high school graduation. She could see the day in clear vivid images. The principal, Mr. Whitestone, had been tanned from his visit to Cape Cod earlier that month. His hair was slicked back as if he had been in a 60s movie and his horn-rimmed glasses shined in the afternoon sun. He sashayed to the podium with much pomp and circumstance, having cleared his throat, he began.

"We are filled with pride for this young lady, who surmounted many difficulties in her life to reach this goal, and without further ado, I give you Ms. Veronica Wheaton, valedictorian, class of 1998." The dean had spoken in a loud, clear voice, then had led everyone in a round of applause that had caused a standing ovation.

Everyone had been so pleased with her achievement. Mom and Uncle Jeb were attending the ceremony, but as Veronica reached the podium to give her speech, she had noticed Uncle Jeb slipping in the back door, and her mother was nowhere to be found. She took a deep breath, putting her disappointment and anger aside. This had been her day and no one was going to ruin it for her. She adjusted the microphone and began her speech.

"We are the promise of tomorrow, the dream that's ready to be born. Whatever your circumstances, whatever horrible things have

happened to you in your life, you have the power to rise above it, and make a new life for yourself. The choice is up to you. If you want to make a difference in this world, leave your mark, use the sour grapes you've been handed, and turn them into a delectable wine, then the ball will be in your court. Will you be brave enough to meet this challenge? No one promised it would be easy, but it IS attainable. Go boldly my fellow graduates!"

Veronica took a sip of water, as she glanced over the crowd; still no Mom, her uncle was sitting in the back of the auditorium alone. She took another sip of water to compose herself, and continued.

"We've heard it before, we are the future, but I say to you, look toward the future and seize the day! Don't look back over what could have been, or should have been. Take each day as a chance to create the world and the life you want to have. Here's to a great and glorious future!"

Then Veronica had lifted her graduation cap in the air, and the students had followed in a rousing cheer and she had been satisfied that, at least, she had had her peers' admiration.

After the graduation, her family had planned to go to dinner to celebrate, but Veronica decided to celebrate on her own. Since her mother couldn't bring herself to show up at her daughter's most important day, then she wasn't going to grace her with a dinner, no matter what lame excuse Uncle Jeb made. Veronica had entered the dressing room to return the cap and gown. Just as she was about to leave, there was a knock on the door. The others were still taking pictures with their families, so she had the place to herself. She opened the door to find Uncle Jeb standing in the hallway.

"Hey, my girl, I'm so proud of you." Uncle Jeb's white beard had tickled Veronica's face, as he leaned in to give her a peck on the cheek.

"Thanks," Veronica said, as she moved away from him.

"Honey, your mother wanted to come; she just got so tired and depressed."

"Yada, yada, yada." Veronica snarled.

"I know we were going to your favorite restaurant to celebrate, but how about we pick up Chinese and go celebrate with your mother," Uncle Jeb tried to hug her, but she pulled away.

"Sorry, Uncle, but I made other plans."

Uncle Jeb's eyes glistened with tears. Veronica had never meant to hurt him, but he had been forever making excuses for her mother, just like Dad had always done. Veronica hadn't waited for his response; she just opened the dressing room door and sprinted out until she had reached the exit to the school. Uncle Jeb had been following in the distance and trying to keep up.

As she reached the parking lot, Uncle Jeb, out of breath, caught up to her. He took several deep breaths before he could speak. Veronica stood there disinterested in her Uncle's distress. Finally, he was able to speak.

"Please, daring girl, don't leave like this."

Veronica had let out a large sigh, and then put her things in the trunk. "Uncle, is this going to take long, I really need to go."

"No, honey. I want to give you this. Remember I will always love you." Uncle Jeb's voice had cracked as he spoke and for a split—second, Veronica had considered having dinner with him.

"I gotta go. Talk to you soon!"

"Aren't you coming back tonight?"

"No, I have to start my internship at the college bookstore right away. I need the money for school. Besides, Cindy's family asked me to spend the night, they are having a party for her." She got in the car, and as she sped off, she yelled out "Bye Uncle!"

Uncle Jeb stood for a moment, trying to compose himself. He had been devastated by Veronica's lack of feeling.

The next morning, before Veronica had driven off to college in Rhode Island, she opened the card her uncle had given her at the school. The note read, "To the smartest girl I know. You're a treasure to me. Go with God." Enclosed in the note was a 100 dollar bill.

"Hmm, go with God, yeah right! Well, at least I got some money to tide me over." Then Veronica got into her car and made her way to Rhode Island, never having looked back again.

After her first year in college, she had secured a job at a diner for the summer, having lived off campus in a boarding house. Uncle Jeb had pleaded for her to spend the summer with him, but she had wanted to forget all that family drama and pain. As the years progressed, she had responded less and less to his invitations, until they came no more.

Now she felt sorry for having left Uncle Jeb hurt and alone on the sidewalk that day, and for cutting him out of her life afterward. The poor man tried to make a happy home for her. He hadn't deserved the blame; then again, maybe her mother hadn't been to blame either. If she had dinner with them that night, as Uncle Jeb had suggested, she may have been able to mend fences, or at least she would have gone off to college without closing off all ties to her family.

But then again, she was a young woman, and all of her life the people who were supposed to protect, and love her, had failed her. *What was I supposed to do?* She once had heard a teacher say that a decision made in haste may cost you dearly in future years. Veronica would never know if that had been true for her on her graduation night.

The need to pray hit Veronica like a flash of lightning. She sat up in bed and began,

"Dear Lord, help me understand all of this. I don't know where to go from here, or how to fix it at this stage of the game. Please help me now."

Then Veronica got an idea, and so she spoke out into the night, "Mom, I'm sorry for leaving, I'm sorry you were incapable of mothering me, but most of all, I'm sorry for this emptiness inside of me for, never having known you, and that you had never really known who I was either."

Veronica felt a strange sensation come over her, just like the one that she had the night she accepted Christ. She sat still on her bed for a minute, trying to figure it all out, when a soft, cool breeze blew through the window, giving Veronica a chill. Then she felt a presence, and heard in her spirit, these words, *you will always be my little girl.*

Without conscious thought, she responded, "I'm sorry, Mom." Then she cried the kind of tears that cleansed, and healed her broken heart, and lulled her to sleep.

CHAPTER FIFTEEN

When Veronica had reached the Medical building on the day of the assessment, Michelle had already been in Dr. McDermott's office, so she took a seat outside. Then the door opened, and Dr. McDermott and Michelle emerged.

"Hey, did you sleep here in the Doctor's office last night?" Veronica joked.

"No, I just got here and—"

Doctor McDermott interrupted. "I was just telling Michelle what to expect."

Veronica glared at the doctor, then squeezed Michelle's hand. "Well, relax, you'll do fine."

"You seem to be full of exuberance this morning."

"Yeah, I had a good night last night."

"Wait here with your friend, while I go to meet Doctor Bookman. Doctor McDermott gave her a reassuring smile, a few minutes later, she returned with Dr. Bookman. "Shall we?" Dr. McDermott opened the door to her office, and Michelle followed her inside.

"I guess we shall." Michelle said, as she turned to look at Veronica before shutting the office door.

"Relax, this will be fine." Veronica gave her a hug.

"Okay, whatever." Michelle shrugged.

They approached Dr. McDermott's desk, a sofa sat on the right side of it. The doctor shook Michelle's hand and then they sat down on the sofa.

"Hello, I'm Dr. Bookman, just pretend this is a conversation between two friends. Dr. McDermott is just here to observe."

Veronica was getting restless waiting for Michelle, it had been a good thirty minutes, so she decided to walk down to the cafeteria, to grab a cup of coffee. As she sipped the coffee, she wondered how Michelle was doing. The doctor seemed very kind, and Veronica hoped it would make a difference in evaluating Michelle.

This felt like old times for her. As a youth she and her Uncle had taken her mother to an evaluation, but that one had not gone well at all, leaving her alone and frightened again.

Whatever was in store for her future, Veronica knew it would be okay—it had to be okay. For now, Veronica needed to concentrate on Michelle; this was her mission, a mission given to her by God. It wasn't an accident that they were put together. Veronica knew it was part of God's plan to restore the two of them, each one helping the other to see things more clearly; to be what God had intended from the moment they were conceived in their mother's womb. That thought proved to be very comforting to her in the weeks, and months ahead, as she forged out a new life.

CHAPTER SIXTEEN

After what had felt like the two longest hours of Veronica's life, Michelle emerged from behind closed doors, laughing and smiling. Dr. Bookman followed behind her. Veronica got up and approached them.

"Well, judging from the expression on your face, it went well."

"Yes, it did," Dr. Bookman patted Michelle on the back.

"That's great!" Veronica's eyes lit up.

"Ms. Wheaton, please step into my office for a minute," Dr. McDermott said.

"Sure, I'll be right with you."

Michelle looked nervous and Veronica tried to relieve her fears. "I'm sure it's just professional courtesy. You know, client/patient confidentiality is in play here."

"Yeah, I know," Michelle sighed.

"Shall we go into my office?" The doctor led the way, Veronica walking behind her.

Veronica closed the door behind her, and sat down on the sofa. "So where do we stand, Dr. McDermott?" Veronica's sapphire eyes lay fixed upon her.

"Doctor Bookman would like your feedback."

Veronica turned to face the doctor. "Okay, so what do you want to know?"

The doctor took a breath and continued. "First off, I believe Michelle is mentally competent; however, at present she is still depressed, probably due to worry over her son, which is common. But I do believe that something, or someone has caused her pain. I don't believe it's recent, in spite of the baby and husband situation."

"I agree. I think something in her childhood, not just with her husband, is creating her fearful disposition. She seems afraid to speak, or even fight for herself."

"Good, so we are on the same page. Ms. Martin expressed a desire to be released into your custody. I can arrange that, if it's alright with you." Doctor Bookman wore a pensive smile.

"Of course, I would love to have Michelle stay with me."

"I'll get to work on it then. Beyond that, I cannot break confidentiality."

Veronica leaned in, her eyes wide. "Of course, I wouldn't expect you to."

"So, here's what I propose. She is doing well here at the hospital clinic. She seems to want her independence, and she considers you a good friend."

"Right, that's true."

"So, I want to see her twice a week for therapy. At least for six months, and then I'll re-evaluate her, and we can proceed for the child custody hearing then." Dr. Bookman leaned back in her chair, waiting for Veronica's response.

"Well, I guess that's reasonable. "Does Michelle know about this?"

"Yes, and she's okay with it, I think she'll be fine, she just needed someone to believe in her."

"Yeah, I'm sure she did," Veronica had a faraway look in her eyes.

"Is everything all right, Ms. Wheaton?"

"Oh yes. I was just thinking about someone I once knew. Michelle reminds me of her."

"Oh and how is she doing?"

"She died a long time ago."

"I'm sorry, can I help?"

"Thanks for the offer, but I'm at peace with it now."

Veronica left the room, and met Michelle. She gave her a big hug and said, "Congratulations!"

Michelle's smile glowed, as she spoke, "Thanks I owe it all to you."

"Well, you wanted to get better, you should be proud of yourself," Veronica's smile filled her face.

"Want to grab a bite to eat in cafeteria?" Veronica looked at Michelle.

"Sure, anything to stay out of that room longer."

"Well, it'll be over soon." Veronica patted her on the back.

Doctor McDermott interrupted. "I hate to break up this happy fest, but she cannot be unescorted just yet."

"Can a nurse, or aid come with us? Veronica asked.

Just then, one of the aides walked by. "John, are you going to lunch? The doctor asked.

"Yes I am." He smiled.

"Will you please escort these two ladies to lunch, and when you're all finished, bring Ms. Martin back to me?"

Then he turned to Michelle, "Shall we go?" He took her by the arm with Veronica on her other side of her.

Michelle sighed. "Right now I'd rather be eating Chinese at Pow Tong's on Broad Street."

"Okay, then when you're released, Pow Tong's it is!" Veronica smiled.

While they waited for their sandwiches, Veronica took the opportunity to talk to Michelle about the doctor's decision.

"Listen, Michelle, it's really great that Dr. Bookman thinks you're capable, and all—"

"But?" Michelle's eyes narrowed.

"But, you have to show you can do well outside the hospital. So, when we return in a few months, you can be totally released, and not in my custody."

"I know that."

"With these custody releases you can work part-time to see how you adjust to everyday life."

"Okay, so I can work at a Quick Mart, or something."

"Yes, but usually the doctor sends you somewhere to work, like in an office, or a store."

"So it will be stated in the custody release?"

"Yes, it will."

"That's great!"

"But, you also need to be open with Dr. Bookman."

"Why are you telling me what I already know?" Michelle's eyes narrowed.

"I want to make sure you know how things will play out for you."

"Oh, I see. Why can't we talk as things come up?"

"Michelle, I have to go back to Rhode Island, and I won't be able to help all the time."

"Yes, of course, I understand," Michelle said in a flat tone of voice."

"I just want you to be more confident in your abilities; that's all."

"I'm not like your mother, Veronica," Michelle snapped.

Veronica recoiled. "I never said that you were."

"But, you think it, don't you? When are you going to deal with your own demons?" Michelle's stare was kind, but firm.

"I'm trying to do that. I will be going to Hillcrest Manor sometime before I leave, in order to get the house on the market."

"You want no part of your heritage?"

"I just can't live here anymore, Michelle."

"What about Sergeant Bishop?"

"We've only been out together three times, and the rest was just business. I wouldn't consider us a couple, and I don't think he does either. We're just two old friends catching up on our lives."

"Sure, that's what it is."

"You think I'm running away?" Veronica's eyes narrowed.

"I don't know, are you?"

"Now she's playing psychiatrist," Veronica huffed.

"I'm just making an observation. The last time I saw the two of you together, it appeared to be more than *friendship* to me, on both your parts."

"And when was that?"

"When we went to court that day, he had come along."

"That was because he handled your case. Besides, I'm not ready to give up my life in Rhode Island. Sometime in the future, if we feel we want more out of our friendship; maybe, but not now."

"Then why sell the house?"

"Because I'm tired of paying taxes on it, and all the upkeep needed to make it livable for me, isn't worth it."

Michelle was quiet, and then she said, "How about I rent it from you, so you can pay your taxes, and do the updating you say it needs."

"It's a big house, Michelle."

"I need a furnished place; you have one, and we both win."

"Let me think about it."

"The demons will leave, if you tell them to, Veronica."

"Oh, you don't say?" Veronica glared at her.

"That's what Dr. Bookman told me."

"Well isn't she a wellspring of knowledge," Veronica smirked.

"Yes, she certainly is," Michelle stared back at her.

CHAPTER SEVENTEEN

Veronica went back to the Inn, having left Michelle at the hospital with the aide, who escorted her back to Doctor McDermott's office. She was mentally exhausted, and needed to rest. Veronica entered her room and went straight to bed. She didn't even bother to change, falling sound asleep in her business suit, and high heels.

Veronica didn't know how long she'd been asleep, or if she was still asleep, because the images dancing before her appeared to be so real. First her father came in view, his face distorted in pain. As he became clearer in Veronica's focus, she noticed he had been crying, and pleading for forgiveness. Veronica screamed, *No, no! You left me without any explanation, except that you would need to concentrate on Mom, but Mom was in the nut house; you could have spent that time with me. I needed you Dad, why did you leave me?* She pounded her fists into her pillow. The motion from her fists brought her to her senses, as she realized what had just happened.

Veronica sat up straight in her bed, sweat poured off her body, like a waterfall on the mountainside.

"Lies, Dad, that's all you were to me, a pack of lies." She circled her room, while shouting into the thin air.

"Michelle says I must face my demons. Well, Dad, you devil of a liar. I'm here, and I know I should give you mercy, but you can't have my m e r c y, not now, maybe not ever!"

The hatred in her voice, frightened Veronica, as she realized she might be falling back into old habits. The possibility that this might be happening, caused her to fall on her knees and weep. During the mourning of her soul, God whispered, "How many times must you forgive your brother?" Veronica, feeling humbled, and broken, then whispered through her tears, "seventy times seven."

A sweet stillness, covered in peace enveloped the room, and entered her troubled soul. She sat back on her heels, and clutching her pounding heart, whispered into the air, "I forgive you Daddy, for everything."

A fragrant scent filled the air, and tickled Veronica's nose, which she recognized as God's redeeming love. She had heard of others who experienced God that way, even her friend, Roy, when he was converted, and now it was happening to her. She knelt down for a moment and prayed, "What do I do, Lord?" As she meditated; it calmed her down, and she fell back to sleep, right there on the floor.

The purge of her soul continued. This time she had been transported to a place in her youth. Suddenly, she felt as if she was in a remake of the Christmas Carol, as her mother, dressed in a beautiful white dress, pranced before her eyes. Veronica recognized the dress as her mother's wedding dress.

"Mom, what's happening to me?" Veronica called to her.

"Be happy, be brave!' she heard in her spirit.

"But, Mom, what do you mean by that?" Veronica called again.

Then her mind's eye watched her mother climb into the attic of Uncle Jeb's house, and open an old, worn-out cedar chest. "It's all in here for you, my baby," she said, as she faded away.

Veronica woke up, shivering on the cold, wooden floor. She reached for her robe, and then checked the time on the clock; it was 4:15 AM. She wanted, and needed to speak with Roy, but it was too early to wake him up. Veronica moved toward the kitchen, and made a cup of coffee, as she sipped it, her body became more chilled and icy.

This feeling frightened her; maybe she was having a breakdown. All the information she read on bipolar disorder said that the disease could be inherited. *Did it skip her, and she received her father's genetic inheritance, as she hoped, or was this episode the beginning of her worst fear?*

She checked the time again; it was 4:50 AM. Veronica decided she needed to call Roy now, if she was having a breakdown, she didn't want to be alone.

"Hello?" A groggy Roy said.

"Hey, Roy, it's Veronica."

"Wha, what's wrong?"

"I'm sorry to wake you."

"What's wrong, Veronica?"

"Roy, I I…" Veronica sobbed into the telephone.

"What's happened, honey?"

"I think I'm having a nervous—", she gasped.

"You think you're having a nervous breakdown?"

"Yeah, and I'm scared."

"Okay, don't do anything, Veronica, just try to relax and I'll be there in a couple of hours."

"Thank you, Roy…I—"

"It will be okay, Veronica, I'll be there soon. God is with you."

Veronica hung up. She felt better now that Roy was on his way. Veronica thought back on how only a few months ago she hated him, and his Christian ways, and all that love and forgiveness talk. Now she knew he would be the key to her sanity. He could put things in the proper perspective. Veronica believed he was sent to help her find her way.

But, would God allow me to fall apart, just like my mother? What purpose could that serve? But, then, I deserve it for being so unkind to people. Nevertheless, Roy always says "God is love," so why would He torture me, when I'm sorry for my behavior?

Veronica took the Bible off the counter, and opened it to find that Roy's book was hidden between the pages. The title glistened in the moonlight rays. *"I Have Loved You with an Everlasting Love."*

At that moment Veronica knew things would be okay. God was in control, and He loved her, no matter what happened.

"Roy, who was that?" his wife said.

"It was Veronica Wheaton, honey."

"What's wrong now?" Carol said in a strained tone of voice.

"Honey, she's a new Christian. She needs support; you remember how it was for us."

"Yes, I do but—"

"Honey, I love only you, but Veronica's in a bad way, and with her background, well I don't know what could happen."

"Do you think she'll hurt herself?"

"No, at least I hope not. That's why I have to go."

"I know, Roy. I'll be here praying for you both."

"Thanks, baby," Roy kissed his wife tenderly on the lips, then headed for his car.

Roy entered the New England Thruway toward Connecticut, then onto I-287. He seemed to be gliding along, making record time. "I guess it's too early for commuters," he told himself.

Then he prayed into the early morning air, "Lord, I have no idea what I'll find, when I get to Veronica's place. Whatever it is, prepare my heart, and my words, and give me wisdom."

Roy continued on I-287 until he approached the sign welcoming him to Tarrytown, New York, "The Place of the Sleepy Hollow Legend."

Roy recalled the story from his youth; Ichabod Crane from Sleepy Hollow, a schoolmaster, turned into a headless horseman; a popular legend of this town, and a classic favorite Halloween story. What added to the legend, was the site of the Old Dutch church built by Frederick Philipse that still stood like a proud peacock today.

Perhaps it was appropriate that this town, filled with its rich history, and haunting legends, had also been the place that brought so much pain, and haunting misery to Veronica's life. Now, however, it may be the very place she would find her redemption, as she strived to unravel her own family's haunted secrets.

CHAPTER EIGHTEEN

Roy approached the driveway for the Inn, where Veronica was staying. Then he took his cell phone out to call her.

"Hey, I'm in the lobby."

"Okay, I'll come down in a minute."

Veronica's voice sounded shaky, as if she had been crying all this time.

Roy sat in an antique loveseat, and perused the magazines on the table in front of him. Then Veronica entered the room, looking like a worn–out shoe, all wrinkled up and used; her eyes swollen and red.

"Hey, Roy thanks for coming. Let's go upstairs to talk."

"Sure, hon. Are you okay?"

"I'm just completely exhausted, Roy. Emotionally and spiritually confused."

They entered the elevator, neither one saying a word on the way up to her room. When they entered the suite, Roy went to the sofa, and sat down.

"So do you want to tell me what this is all about?"

"I'm not sure myself. All I know is that I'm not the same girl I used to be; confident and unafraid. Now, I worry about everything. Mostly about other people, and I keep having these nightmares, or visions about my family."

"Well, it sounds like God is healing your bruised emotions; possibly He's trying to show you the truth about your family."

"But, I feel like I'm losing my mind. I thought coming to Christ would be such a joyful thing."

"It is, but you have things that need fixing. Unless you face them, you can't move forward. Do you remember the story of Lot's wife from the Bible? She kept looking back to her past, until she was destroyed by it."

"Gee, what a bad break for her."

"Well, there is a lot of truth in that story; for you it's like peeling an onion."

"How's that?" Veronica frowned.

"Well, when you peel an onion, you cry, but the taste of the onion on a burger, or in a salad is worth the tears."

"Oh, I get it. So I can't be free to enjoy, until I peel the onion of my past."

"Something like that."

"What of these freaky dreams? I mean, my mom was like that, and I'm—"

"You're afraid you've got her sickness."

"Yes, that's it."

"Can you share the dreams?"

"Yes, I can, that's what I wanted to tell you, so maybe you can help me figure it all out."

"Well, it's for you to figure out, but I can help guide you, and give a listening ear."

"Whatever help you can give, I trust you, Roy."

"The one that bothers me the most, is when I saw my mother. She was wearing a white gown, but she looked a little tortured, then she told me to "be *happy, be brave!*'"

Then I watched her go to the attic of Uncle Jeb's house. She opened a cedar chest, and said, 'It's all in here for you.' That's it; she disappeared. Then I called you."

He shrugged, as if unmoved by what he just heard. "So is there a cedar chest in the attic?"

"I don't know. I haven't been up there in years."

"Maybe you should find out."

"This doesn't freak you out? You think this is real then?" Veronica looked astonished.

"It could be, Veronica. It's been known to happen. God does communicate in our dreams. The way to your freedom could rest in that cedar chest."

"If it exists," she shrugged.

"Well, there's only one way to find out."

"I don't think I can just yet."

"Ask God to prepare you, and He will."

"Roy, do you think I'm helping Michelle because I'm trying to work off the guilt of not understanding my mother?"

"I don't know, but if you are, God put you two together for a reason."

"Michelle needs a place to live, and she wants to rent Hillcrest Manor from me."

"And that makes you uncomfortable?"

"I was going to sell the place, but—"

"You're confused, and that's understandable, so perhaps if you find the cedar chest, you'll have your fears relieved."

"What if there's no cedar chest?"

"It doesn't alter the fact that God is trying to communicate with you. Maybe it's symbolic, whatever the case, you will have an answer."

"Well, you know more about these things than I do." Veronica let out a heavy sigh.

"Let me pray with you."

Roy took her hands in his and then bowed his head.

"Dear Lord, help Veronica to find the truth, and when she does, let it be a complete release for her. Give her direction and guidance, and send someone into her life that can add some answers to her questions. Lord, help her to know she is not her mother, but a unique, separate individual created by you. Amen."

"Roy, thank you so much for everything," Veronica sniffled.

"You're welcome, sweetie. I need to head back home now. If I'm lucky I'll get there just when Carol is having her morning coffee."

"Give her my thanks for letting you come today."

"I will, Veronica, trust where God leads you, and remember that he has your back."

CHAPTER NINETEEN

Veronica had begun to notice positive changes in her behavior since that night when Roy had come to help her. She was experiencing the joyful transformation of being a Christian, a despicable idea just a few months ago. However, this newly discovered treasure, and peacefulness was the only real thing that kept her from self-destruction.

The transformation process also altered her nightly routine. She used to drink a glass of wine while watching the daily news, and cast judgment on the other journalist's reporting styles.

Now her routine consisted of drinking warm tea while reading the Bible that she had recently purchased at a local Christian store, and asking God to guide her steps. Her entire focus changed from a self-centered, ambitious person, to a compassionate news reporter, caring for fragile, Michelle Martin, victim of a failed system.

There were still bumps along the road, and setbacks in her walk, as the old Veronica reared its ugly head every now and again, but the good thing was that she despised the old Veronica, as much as she loved the new one. She remembered how many times Roy told her, "Nothing in life is easy, not even conversion. Just pray and eventually everything will come together."

But for old Veronica, everything was either black or white. The new Veronica experienced everything through a broader lens, and she was no longer master of her own ship, instead she was led by a greater source. This was not easy for Veronica, who was used to leading, and not following. At times, when frustrations overwhelmed her, she contemplated giving it all up, but then what?

She knew deep down inside, that in order to accomplish the desired transformation, she must unconditionally surrender her will to God. Until then, Veronica kept plodding along, hoping and praying she'd eventually get accustomed to not being in the driver's seat of her life.

On another note, she needed to get busy and clean up the place, because Michelle was coming to stay with her for a while. The assessment had gone well, and Dr. Bookman recommended Michelle be released in Veronica's care for six months. She needed to have a job to show she could support herself. Then go back to the doctor for re-evaluation for the competency hearing.

Veronica assessed the situation. "I'd better put my clothes away, so she could at least sit down." She snickered.

"I have that job interview set up for her that Doctor Bookman recommended in her assessment report; I hope she gets it. But I think the interview is just a formality, its understood by the agreement that the job is hers; unless she truly blows the interview." Veronica waved her hand in dismissal. "She'll get the job. It's only at the Quick-Mart, but it's a start."

Veronica got into her car, then drove to the hospital to pick up Michelle. She walked down the hallway, and to the left toward the admissions desk.

"Hey, Janie, how's it going? she said, sporting a big friendly smile.

"Oh, great, you're here for Michelle, right?"

"Yes, I am."

"She's going to do just great, I know it. Have you found that husband yet?" Janie, the admissions clerk added.

"I found his address in Staten Island, but every time I go there, he's never around. I think he knows somehow, that he's a wanted man," Veronica smirked.

"How do you mean?"

"Well, if he has any conscience, he might be feeling guilty, so inside, he is a haunted man, always on the run."

"Yeah, but you'll get him; look at all you've done for Michelle."

"Thanks for the vote of confidence," Veronica smiled.

Just then, Michelle Martin emerged into the hallway looking happier and more confident than Veronica had ever seen her.

"Hey Michelle, you look great!" Veronica patted her on the back.

"Thanks, I'm ready to start over, thanks to you."

"Well, let's get going." Veronica took Michelle's suitcase and the two women headed for the car. Veronica stopped her just before the exit door, and said, in a low tone of voice," Michelle the news media is out there; don't be afraid, I'll do the talking, okay?"

"What are they doing here? You said you were my friend, why did you tell the news?" Michelle tensed up.

"I was assigned by my boss to cover you, maybe he sent the crew, although I wouldn't think—"

"So you sold me out!" she cried.

"No, no I didn't, I never sent my story."

"So how come this?" Michelle pointed to the reporters outside the hospital.

"I'm sure it's some other reporters. My boss knows how I feel about the situation. However, in this business anybody could get a hold of your information. If I had to make a wild guess, that's what's happening now. Just stick with me, I promise you, that it will be fine."

Michelle let out a sigh, and then held onto Veronica's arm, as they exited the building.

As soon as they were standing outside of the building, a cavalcade of reporters flooded their space, pressing cameras in their faces, as well as microphones.

"Please, give Ms. Martin her space!" Veronica shouted.

"Ms. Martin, how do you feel, now that you've been declared sane?"

"How would you feel if someone declared you insane because you had a rough break in life?" Veronica snarled.

The young reporter backed off. Then another one approached her.

"Ms. Martin, what are you plans for the future?"

"Right now, Ms. Martin is going home to start a new job, and that's all the questions we will answer." Veronica's sapphire eyes pierced the young man's glance, and he backed off.

Veronica pulled Michelle's arm into a tight grip, then whispered to her, "just look straight ahead and walk fast. I've got you covered."

When they entered the car, Veronica exhaled. "Whew! What a bunch of vultures. To think I used to enjoy doing that." She shook her head in disbelief.

"Thanks for helping me out there."

"Don't mention it. Let's just get you home."

The ride back to Veronica's suite had been uneventful. What a blessing it had been to have no media chasing them, and no reporters outside the hotel. Michelle unpacked and Veronica put a set of sheets and towels on the sofa.

"It's not much, but it's comfortable. I've fallen asleep on it once or twice myself," Veronica shrugged.

"Oh, it's fine," Michelle's tone was reserved.

"What's wrong?" Veronica asked.

"It's just—"

"Just, what?"

"Have you found my husband? I mean, what if he finds out where I'm staying?"

"We are actively looking for him, but nothing just yet. Don't worry about him finding you. I have the place monitored for intruders. There are security cameras everywhere."

"Please, stop looking for him."

"But, why stop?"

"Because I'm sure he will come after me, cameras or not." Michelle shed a tear.

"What's happened to you, Michelle? Veronica squeezed her

shoulder, then sat down on the sofa and Michelle followed, sitting down next to her."

"He and Dad were into counterfeit car parts, and I believe, illegal drugs as well. When I found out about it, I asked them to stop, but that made things worse. Life became unbearable. They tried to make me believe I was crazy and imagined the whole thing."

"You, poor girl!" Veronica's eyes popped out of her head.

"It was awful. I think my drinks were even spiked at one point, but I couldn't prove it."

"So why didn't you go to the police?"

Michelle squirmed in her seat, "and that's when he said he never wanted kids, and if I had a kid, he'd kill it!"

Now Michelle started to cry. "It will be okay, Michelle; I'm beginning to see the big picture here."

Just then, the telephone rang. "Hello, this is Veronica Wheaton."

"It's me, Veronica. What was that circus outside the hospital?"

"Mark, is that you?"

"Yes, who else would it be?"

"I guess local news got ahold of the story."

"It wasn't you?"

"No, Mark, it wasn't," Veronica spoke in a low tone.

"I'm sorry I didn't trust you, but…"

"Hmm, must be someone in the hospital then."

"Well, here's another news flash; Robert Martin saw the news, and freaked out. He shot himself outside the orphanage where the Martin baby was left."

"Is he—?"

"Yes, he's dead."

Veronica took a deep breath, "Well, there is something he is hiding about his father-in-law's business that could land him in jail."

"Look, in view of everything, this case is closed. So you can come back to work."

"Mark, I'd really like to take a leave of absence. I need to find myself."

"What! I thought you would be ecstatic that you are off the hook!"

"Well, I just need——"

"Wait a minute; are you still going to help that girl?" Mark's voice was strained.

"Mark, I have to. If I'm on extended leave, then it's not your problem. Please, I need to do this."

"Well, since you've done a good job with this, I'll approve it; but be careful."

"I will; thanks so much!"

"Sure. I must be crazy for doing this, but you're welcome."

CHAPTER TWENTY

"What's wrong?" Michelle's voice quivered as she spoke.

"I need to tell you something." Veronica sighed, then went over to the sofa and sat down next to Michelle.

"You're scaring me, I know it's some kind of bad news, and I can't handle anything more right now," Michelle's eyes grew wide.

"Michelle, just listen, please? That was my boss. He just found out your husband killed himself, when he saw us on the news, this morning." Veronica held onto Michelle's shaking hand, as she tried to digest the news.

"So, now what happens? My entire case is out the window. They'll say it's my fault." Michelle gave Veronica a soulful look. Her black eyes sunken, and drawn, as those of a much older woman.

"Don't go projecting into the future. First off, he is out of the picture, and secondly, your competency hearing has nothing to do with his suicide, unless you get yourself in a snit again. So let's concentrate on what's important right now, and that's getting Ryan back where he belongs," Veronica rubbed her shoulder.

Michelle's countenance lifted a bit, as she let out a sigh. "I suppose you're right. I don't want to lose now; after all I've come through to get to this point."

"That's the spirit!" Veronica looked into Michelle's eyes and said, "But here's the thing, you need to tell me the entire truth, or I can't help you get your life back."

Michelle didn't move, or speak she just stared at the floor.

"Michelle do you understand me?"

"Yes, I do." Then Michelle took a deep breath and began her story. "I met Robert in high school; he was my first boyfriend. I was seventeen and thought he was so handsome, with his beautiful blue eyes, and jet–black hair. He was a bodybuilder back then, and all the girls loved him."

"So, you two started dating then."

"No, not at first, not in the usual sense of dating. We only saw each other at the school. After school we'd, sneak off for a soda at the local diner. And he was so attentive to me, leaving flowers, and love notes taped to my locker."

"So what happened?"

"My dad was a real strict disciplinarian. I wasn't allowed to go to dances, or date, until I graduated from high school. All my friends talked about the dances, and their boyfriends. I couldn't stand explaining why I didn't date, like the other girls."

"Then Robert came along and appealed to your vulnerabilities."

"Well, you could put it that way."

"I'm sorry. I'm still a reporter at heart. It's a cross I have to bear," she squeezed Michelle's arm.

Michelle took a breath and started again. "Well, Robert made me feel special. He wouldn't take no for an answer. He finally convinced me that we belonged together."

"How long did you secretly date before you married?"

"My entire senior year, and then our relationship took a turn."

"How so?"

"Robert wasn't happy seeing me for an hour after school. He wanted us to be a real couple."

"He wanted to go to the next level?" Veronica's eyes widened.

"Yes, and around that time, he started getting abusive, mostly name-calling."

"Like what?"

"He'd say I was a child and he needed a woman. One time it

had gotten so bad, I pleaded for his understanding, but he turned around, and slapped me instead."

"What happened next?"

"He threatened to tell my father about us. I feared my father more than Robert at that time."

"Did your father start hitting you then?"

"No, no, but he did hit my mom sometimes, and I was afraid he'd be so angry with me, that he would take it out on Mom."

"So you got pregnant?"

"No, we decided to elope. We went to a justice of the peace. At first, I was so happy, even though Robert worked at a gas station for minimal wage, and all we could afford was to rent a trailer at a very run-down trailer park."

"What happened with your father?"

"He disowned me, but stayed in touch with Robert?"

"So, how long before you got pregnant?"

"Well, things got better; Dad saw his potential, and made him assistant manager in his shop. For a while we seemed to be getting along."

"So, then what happened?"

"Things started to change; he didn't seem content any more. He started calling me names, and slapping me all the time. But then he'd turn and he'd be tender, and kind, like when I first met him. His behavior became very irratic."

"That's when you got pregnant?"

"Yes. I thought he'd be happy, because he always said he wanted a son, but it only made him angry."

"Why do you think he changed his mind about having a famiy?"

"Looking back now, I don't think he ever wanted a child, it was just something he said to get me to run away with him."

"So when things got worse, out of desperation, you gave the child away, right?" Veronica's sapphire eyes pierced Michelle's heart.

"No! I didn't give away my baby. I loved him!" Michelle sobbed uncontrollably now.

"It's okay. So Robert gave the baby away."

"Yes! He said he killed him, although I never thought he'd really kill the baby!"

"He told you he would kill the baby?"

"Yes, And when I got really depressed, and asked questions about Ryan, Robert started taking me to his doctor, telling him that we never had a baby, and he prescribed the pills, and finally, the institution."

"Of course he did, what a perfect setup!" Veronica shook her head.

"What do you mean?"

"Honey, Robert declares you unfit, you get sent away; he's off the hook. Do you know anything about his doctor?"

"No, only they were childhood friends."

"Hmm, how convenient."

"But, what about the medical tests? The reports indicated I was unstable."

"I can't be sure, but I would venture to say the doctor...shall we say...did your husband a little favor. Besides, the new assessment should override that one."

"You think so?"

"I do. Where is that 'so-called' doctor now?"

"He died a few years ago from a boating accident."

Veronica's eyes grew wide. "I do smell a rat here. It's too bad your husband killed himself. I wouldn't be surprised if he also had something to do with that boating accident."

"What good would that do now?" Michelle wiped a tear from her eye.

"Honey, in a few months, when we clear your mental health record, and with your husband gone, you might get Ryan back. As far as I know, your baby is still with a foster family. When we get that certification on your health, the judge will rule in your favor, they always try to rule on the mother's side, when possible."

"But I haven't started the job yet."

"Yes, that's true, but in a few weeks, we can establish that you're working. It's not the greatest situation, but it shows you're making an effort."

"You think it can work?"

"Well, we're certainly going to try," Veronica said, giving Michelle a warm, and reassuring smile.

CHAPTER TWENTY-ONE

The morning sun shimmered through the hotel suite windows, creating brilliant rays of light, on the shiny wood floors. Veronica sat on a balcony chair, drinking in the warmth of the sun. She felt at peace with herself, but not quite ready to face Hillcrest Manor, and the roots of her sorted life, that may rest in its dusty attic.

But then, what if the answer wasn't there? Roy said God was speaking to me anyway. Can I really believe that? For now, she could not entertain that thought.

She closed her eyes for a moment, as events from her life at Hillcrest Manor danced in her head. Then a scene of her, and a little boy walking at the river's edge, came into view. The boy looked familiar, but she could not place him. She seemed to be enjoying his company, and somehow, she knew they were good friends.

It was so real, she could almost see the poppies and other wildflowers blowing in the breeze, that graced the pathway, that led to the Hudson River's edge. The taste of the salty water appeared to be on her lips. Then the scene closed in on the river, and the mysterious figure became clear—it was Brent Bishop!

Memories that had been tucked away in her mind for what felt like centuries, rose to the surface. Brent had been her childhood friend. She recalled that she confided her most intimate secrets to him, and he always listened with keen interest.

Veronica recalled how interesting Brent had been, with his ambitions for the future. It seemed being in law enforcement had always been in his blood. Back then, Brent dragged her to every police spy movie that hit the big screen. As they grew older, and Brent became the captain of the football team, girls flocked to him like pigeons at a park fountain. She was tossed aside like yesterday's news, or so she thought. About that time, her mother had returned from the hospital, and when she had seen that Veronica was no longer with Brent, she had been quite pleased, even though she tried to hide that fact.

But Veronica had always known when her mother wasn't being genuine. Uncle Jeb had tried to run interference, but her mother always managed to create a scene. Veronica recalled that at one time, before she went into the hospital, Brent came to pick her up for a movie, they had been around 14 years old at the time. Veronica's mom walked to the front door with a glass vase in hand. In a fit of anger, she spew out several curse words, then flung the vase at Brent's face, cutting him right above the left eye. As memory had served her, Uncle Jeb had just walked in from the store and seeing Brent bleeding, rushed him to the hospital.

When Veronica and Uncle Jeb confronted her about her behavior, she called them liars, saying she had done nothing of the sort, and that she had had only good feelings for Brent. After that day Brent hadn't come around anymore, and at school he had acted cool around her, and she couldn't blame.

It's strange how the mind works. Before she'd given her life to Christ, she'd forgotten all about this incident, only having remembered Brent as a playboy, who had broken her heart. The truth was apparently too painful to remember, so changing things around in her mind helped her cope.

"What a fool I've been. Brent's only been kind and I've been torturing him by being difficult."

Perhaps it wasn't too late to mend broken fences. Veronica was ready to face her demons now. She would go to Brent's workplace and try to make amends.

She dressed and got into her rental car, driving down the

Thruway to the Tarrytown Police Department. She entered the building, and went up to the reception desk.

"Hello, is Sergeant Bishop in?"

"I'll check," the young police officer picked up the telephone.

"Tell him, Veronica—."

"I know who you are," she smirked.

Veronica felt embarrassed. She caused quite a scene the last time she was here. Things had certainly changed in just a few short weeks. She sat down, and tried to blend in with the other visitor, taking a magazine, and burying her face in it.

"Hello, can I help you?" a familiar voice said.

Veronica put the magazine down, and faced a grinning Brent.

"Hi, Brent, can we talk?"

"Step into my office, please," he said, as he ushered her down the hallway.

"Brent, I need to clear something up," she bit the side of her lip.

"Okay, so I'm listening."

"I've been having flashbacks to my childhood. It seems you were a big part of my life. I think I've blocked out a lot because of... well, the way I was raised."

"How does that involve me?"

"I've been going over past events in my head, to make some sense of it all, and I recall a time when my mother injured you." She waited, holding her breath for his response.

"I've put that behind me," he waved his hand in dismissal.

"But I haven't. I only wanted to say, I'm sorry and I understand why you didn't come back for me, like you promised."

"So that's it?"

"Yes, I only wanted to apologize for my family," Veronica got up and started to leave.

Brent followed her, grabbing her arm. "I accept your apology."

As they left Brent's office, Veronica breathed a sigh of relief that Brent had not made a big deal out of her need to set things right.

"There's a great soup and salad place on Placid Street. It's a stone's throw from here. Are you up for that?"

"It's a good day for soup, given this drizzly weather we're having. It goes right to my bones." Veronica pulled her sweater around her body.

"You need to take some Vitamins to build up your strength." Brent pinched her arm.

Veronica stared him down. "No, thank you."

"So what's going on with you, Veronica? Why are you so anxious to apologize now?"

Veronica took a deep breath; apparently this wasn't over just yet. "I've... I've been having a kind of rebirth. I've accepted Jesus Christ, and since then, things are becoming clearer."

"So, okay, I hear you," he looked into her eyes.

"I know this seems all so strange to you, but I need to make things right, or else I'll have no peace."

"I understand that, I'm a Christian too."

"That's wonderful. When did it happen for you?"

"In the academy, I had a near death experience that changed my life."

"Oh, Cop stuff?"

"No, booze stuff," he grinned.

"Oh, I see," she chuckled.

"Veronica, are you aware that your mother came to my house, and swung a pot at my mom?"

"No, I hadn't known that."

"It was after I had gone to the prom with Alisa Dunlap."

"Why had that mattered?"

"Apparently, she had wanted me to take you, after all."

"What?" Veronica's eyes narrowed.

"She was nuts, Veronica. It wasn't your fault."

"I know that. I've finally made peace with it. But there's something else," she took a deep breath.

"What else?"

"There may be another part of my life's puzzle hidden in an old cedar chest, in the attic at Hillcrest Manor."

"So, are you going to find out if there is another piece to the puzzle?"

"I can't just yet. I'm not ready to face it alone. And then there is the possibility that there isn't another piece, and it may make me feel even worse. But my friend, Roy says I have to face it, either way."

"I think your friend is right. You can't go forward, until you're sure."

"You sound just like him."

"Oh really, is there something else you want to tell me?" he smirked.

"No, he's just a friend from work. Anyway, I don't want to dig up some more family skeletons. God knows there are many," she waved her hand in dismissal.

"Your friend is right, though, regardless of what happens. I can tell you what my mom told me about your family, if it would help."

"Sure, it would, at least it can't hurt at this point."

"Your mom and dad met in college. Your mother was gorgeous, just like you; all the boys loved her. She had been flirtatious, but most men had backed off after they witnessed her Dr. Jekyll and Mr. Hyde personality. But your dad was different; he had been a loner. Not a football hero, not a nerd, just a regular Joe. He was a senior at the time, she, a freshman. Mom said Ben used to watch your mother from afar, never flirting back. Then one day she had asked him what his problem was, and he said, 'I'm in love with you,' and she answered, 'so marry me, you idiot' and so he did."

"Wow! He must have been some glutton for punishment." Veronica's eyes grew wide as she continued, "Do you know anything about my dad's family?"

"He had grown up in a foster home, that's all we know."

"I don't know why he would have kept that a secret."

"Perhaps he had been embarrassed, feeling you would have thought less of him"

"Well, I guess he hadn't known any different about love or marriage, growing up in foster care. But what I don't understand is why he disappeared, leaving me alone," she sighed.

"Is that what you were told?"

"Uncle Jeb said he disappeared that night, when he and his lady friend, Millie, came into my room. But something about that night never sat well with me. There had been a lot of talking downstairs. Someone else had been in the house, but I couldn't recognize the voice. A few years later I had gotten up the nerve to confront Uncle Jeb and I told him I wanted to go find my dad. I told Uncle Jeb I knew he had lied to me. Uncle Jeb had said he was sorry for lying, but he was only trying to protect me. In reality, what happened was he had been killed while driving a pickup truck somewhere in the Midwest."

"Well, I'm not sure that's accurate."

"I never thought so either, but I had been in too much pain to try to find out the truth back then, and that constant lying by Uncle Jeb baffled me. He had always been so honest about everything. Do you know if Dad is living somewhere?"

"I don't know; I only remember Mom saying he'd finally had had enough and she wasn't surprised that he had taken off."

"I wonder where he is, and why the lies?" Tears fell freely from Veronica's eyes.

"Well, maybe he had taken off originally, but later on Uncle Jeb found out where he was living.

"Now I need to find that cedar chest more than ever."

"I'll come with you if you like," Brent squeezed her hand.

"You would do that, after all my family and I have done to you?"

"The Good Book says we have to forgive our brothers no matter what."

"Thank you, Brent, I truly appreciate it."

"Just tell me when you want to go, and I will make sure I'm available."

"Well, how about Saturday afternoon. I need a few days to settle things in my mind, and to check on Michelle."

"That's fine. How are things with her?"

"It's going okay, but the custody case is up in three months, and she needs to be more settled."

"So, Hillcrest Manor might be the right thing for her; just the thing she needs to show her stability."

"Maybe so, only time will tell," Veronica sighed

"I'm sure God will work all things out for your good, and Michelle's, as well."

"Yeah, I'm sure He will."

CHAPTER TWENTY-TWO

After saying their goodbyes at the police station, Veronica walked to her car, and then drove back down the road that led to the hotel. As she neared the hotel entrance, apprehension crept up her spine, just at that moment, the dreaded thought of being alone in her suite entered in. On a moment's impulse, she placed her foot on the gas, and sped right past the entrance, not stopping until she was in front of her old high school. She parked the car, and walked down toward the entrance. Finding a bench under an old oak tree, that faced the main entrance, she sat down. As she reflected on things, she overheard some girls talking about their Friday night dates; comparing notes, and making jokes, as they headed toward the bus stop located on the left side of the parking lot.

Her mind traveled back to the days leading to prom night. In an instant, as if struck by lightning, all seemed clear now. Veronica had been so obnoxious, and needy, that she couldn't blame Brent for canceling their prom date. Seeing from that perspective, if she had been Brent, she would have acted the same way. Veronica snapped back into reality by the sound of the bus wheels, screeching to a halt at the sidewalk's edge of the parking lot. She walked back to her car, and then drove off.

She continued driving along the Hudson River, until she stopped at a small park by the river. Veronica parked the car, and then meandered along the river bank, to collect her thoughts. In the distance stood the Tapanzee Bridge that connected the Hudson River counties to each other, and eventually into New Jersey.

As she stepped over river stones, the sound of the river flowing brought memories of her mother's birthday party at that very same park. Veronica had been thirteen years old, and had spent all morning baking chocolate chip cookies for the celebration in the park. She had been so excited, she couldn't wait to give them to her Mom. Things had been going better at home. Uncle Jeb's store was doing quite well, and Mom had spent her afternoons helping him out. Veronica always stopped there after school, and Uncle Jeb would make her an ice cream soda. It was a special time, when they had bonded as family, but it had all changed that fateful day in June.

Mom had made egg salad sandwiches and Uncle Jeb filled the cooler with ice tea, but Veronica had kept the cookies hidden, she wanted them to be a surprise. Then the three of them piled into Uncle Jeb's station wagon. Veronica counted the minutes until it was time for lunch, folding and re-folding her napkin; she couldn't wait to give her mother the cookies.

It had been a perfect day for a picnic. The weather was warm, and the cool breeze had blown wonderful summer scents of fresh grass, and fragrant flowers from along the River bank. Mom had seemed very happy, almost loving, and Veronica had thought it would stay that way forever. Then Uncle Jeb had poured everyone some more ice tea and said, "Veronica, don't you have a surprise for your mother?"

"You got me a surprise? Well, how lovely," Mom said, while patting her on the back.

"Oh, yes Mom, I know you'll just love them." Veronica smiled from ear to ear.

Then Veronica took the cookies from her bag, and placed them in front of her mother. She had carefully wrapped them in plastic wrap, tying them neatly with a bright red ribbon, Mom's favorite color. Veronica had placed the cookies in front of her and said, "Happy birthday, Mom. I hope you enjoy them."

Her mother then stared at the cookies for a good solid minute, sporting a look of disappointment, mingled with disgust, and said, "Cookies? This is what you give me for a gift, a bunch of stupid cookies?" Then she pulled off the ribbon, and loosened the plastic wrap, tossing them onto the grass, where they had broken, and scattered over the lawn.

"Your daughter made these cookies herself," Uncle Jeb had pleaded with her to have compassion, as he drew Veronica close to him.

"Well, it's about time she got domesticated. I was beginning to think I had a son, instead of a daughter."

Veronica had been horrified; she broke away from Uncle Jeb and ran toward an old Elm tree, sliding down its trunk and onto the ground, and cried. Her sobs were so loud, Uncle Jeb ran to comfort her. Looking back at her mother, he said, "You disgust me. You should be grateful for this little one. I know I am." Then he grabbed Veronica and held her to his chest.

Veronica's mom began to sob and said, "Well, you know it's my sickness; I can't help it."

"You know what? I'm just sick to death of you using that for an excuse to hurt this poor baby girl."

And on that note, Uncle Jeb had taken Veronica home, leaving her mother alone in the park. That had been the first time she recalled, that Uncle Jeb got in between her, and one of Mom's manic fits. Several hours later, when her mother still hadn't showed up, Uncle Jeb called the police. They brought Veronica's mother home, half dazed. Then Uncle Jeb took Mom back to the hospital and that's where she had stayed for quite some time.

Veronica got back into her car, and drove to Orchid Street, where Uncle Jeb once had his general store. The shops, some historic landmarks from the eighteenth century, still kept their historic integrity, but for the most part, nothing seemed the same as when she was a young girl. She drove a little further down the tree lined boulevard, until she came to the place where her uncle's store once stood. Now a grocery store took its place.

A deep sadness fell on Veronica. Seeing that the place that once housed a wonderland of treats, no longer existed caused her pain. She loved her Uncle Jeb, and, until this moment, she did not realize how much he had done to give her a safe, loving home. Tears fell from her eyes, as she recalled being on an assignment when he died. The old man called for her, but she just couldn't tear herself away from the next big scoop.

"I'm sorry Uncle Jeb. Thank you for all you tried to do for me," Veronica sobbed openly in front of the store. As she stood in her grief, she felt a hand on her shoulder, it was Michelle.

"Veronica, are you okay?"

"What are you doing here, Michelle? Veronica wiped the tears from her eyes.

"I'm on my lunch hour and thought I'd pick up some groceries to cook dinner for us tonight, and Dewey's has the best rib-eye steaks in town."

"Oh, that's nice." Veronica said in a low tone of voice.

"What's wrong? Why are you crying?"

"It's just that Dewey's used to be my uncle's general store. There used to be an old-fashioned soda fountain, and candy store, with groceries of every kind. Every day after school, he'd make an ice cream soda for me. I never realized how much he did for me until now."

"I'm sure, he understands. You were just a kid, and had a lot of pain inside of you."

"I wish I could believe that," Veronica said, as she trembled.

"Let's go have a cup of coffee in the diner across the way," Michelle said as she led Veronica to the diner. When they were seated, Veronica opened up her heart.

"Michelle, you really don't know a lot about me."

"Well, you didn't know about me, but that didn't stop you from helping me."

"I think you may have been right. I had to ease my conscious by helping you."

"Veronica, you're not super woman. You're human, and a lot of that bad stuff happened when you were a helpless kid."

"I know, I know that, but still—" Veronica stared out of the diner window, in a daze.

"Look, Veronica, you've been great with me; because of you I got a job, and today I found a new job, as a bank teller."

"You did!"

"Yes, and it's because you believed in me."

"Well, you wanted it to begin with."

"Not at first, but now I can see a future for me, and hopefully my son."

"That's great Michelle, I'm happy for you."

"You'll be happy too someday."

"I'm not so sure," Veronica sighed.

"Is this about Brent Bishop?"

"What makes you say that?" Veronica's eyes got big.

"You like him, I can tell."

"Brent and I were childhood sweethearts."

"So, that's great that you found each other again."

"I don't know about finding each other like that right now. I can't really think of anything, but just a friendship, and with my–"

Michelle put her hand up to quiet Veronica. "Before you say another word; he knows your history, I presume, so let yourself be loved."

"He knows some things, but—."

"Sometimes we have to go through a lot of muck before we find true love, but it's out there, for everybody if you're opened to it. I'm not giving up on it either, to spite what's happened to me. I want my baby to have a daddy someday too." Michelle smiled, as she reflected on that thought.

"Well, first I have to settle my family issues, and I still have a job in Rhode Island. I have to figure out what I want to do about that."

"We have newspapers here in case you hadn't noticed."

"Very funny; there's something Brent is going to help me with. When that's settled, I'll be able to make a decision."

"Well, I hope it works out for you."

"Thanks, Michelle. On another note, have you heard anything about the hearing?"

"Yes, it's September eighteenth. With my new job, I can look for a place before the hearing."

"Well, if you're still interested in Hillcrest Manor, I might be willing to rent."

"Oh sure, but don't do it just for me."

"I'm not; I think I need to keep the place. Uncle Jeb would have wanted that. Besides, the basement has a full apartment, and its own entrance to the backyard."

"Oh, that sounds great."

"If I do move back here, I'll be able to live in the house. You'll have a built in babysitter," Veronica laughed.

"Great! When can I see it?"

"Let's say Sunday afternoon?"

"Sounds great to me!"

"Thanks, Michelle for everything."

"Thank you for believing in me."

Michelle and Veronica left the diner. Michelle gave the groceries to her, so she could put them in the fridge. She still had a couple of hours to work before going home, having met Veronica, saved her the trip of bringing the groceries home on her lunch break.

Veronica headed back to the Inn. After the dinner with Michelle, she excused herself early. Her head was splitting, but she didn't sleep much that night. Her mind kept wandering back to the cedar chest.

Did the cedar chest exist? And if it did, what was in it? Will I find the peace I'm looking for, or just another puzzle to put together? What about Brent, and Heritage World News? Could I leave my job and start a real relationship at this stage of my life, and with all my emotional baggage still in need of healing?

Her life was changing, there were so many choices before her; so many unanswered questions, that it made her head spin. Only God could get her through this mess; only God knew the beginning from the end, and only He would help her make the right choices, and find the right answers to her questions.

CHAPTER TWENTY-THREE

The sun shone through Veronica's bedroom window, ushering in a new day, the day that could change her fate forever. She was nervous, and afraid, all at once. *What if there is no cedar chest?* Veronica felt her body tremble. No, she wouldn't entertain that thought; she would go forward in faith. Besides, Brent would be there with her for moral support, whatever the outcome.

Veronica took a steamy, hot shower. The water massaged her weary bones, but her mind was still racing. *What if this was some kind of illusion, like the kind her mother used to have during an episode?* She did not know enough about that part of her mother's illness, to make an educated assessment, so she prayed she'd have the courage to face whatever was ahead.

She heard a knock at the door, just as she tied her robe, and sat down to a cup of coffee.

"Good morning," Brent's cheerful greeting put Veronica at ease.

"I brought breakfast." He held up a bag of bagels, and another with butter and cream cheese.

"Come in. I just made coffee."

"I hope you don't mind that I've come so early. I thought you'd like the early morning support."

"Oh, I don't mind at all; this way we can go earlier, and get it over with."

"Sure, whatever you want to do."

"Thanks, Brent, for everything. You've been a true friend."

"Don't mention it. Have you settled things with Michelle?"

"Yeah, I'm going to keep Hillcrest Manor. She'll rent the basement apartment. I haven't decided yet about the rest of the house, if I rent it out, or move back. It depends on whether I stay in my current job."

"Are you thinking of leaving?" Brent asked.

"I'm toying with the idea."

"Well, I hope you vote in favor of moving here. I know Michelle would love it, and so would I."

"Brent, I can't promise you anything right now. I'm so unsettled."

"I understand. No pressure at all. Take your time to think things through."

Veronica sighed, and then got up from the table. I'll be ready in a few minutes. Make yourself comfortable."

Veronica left the room. She dressed in an old pair of jeans and sweatshirt, pulling her hair back in a ponytail. She didn't bother with makeup. This was going to be a messy day, in more ways than one, and she was sure her emotions would run roughshod. She glanced in the mirror, "Not exactly a beauty queen, but, so what." Then she left the room.

"Okay, Brent I'm ready, aren't I a real beauty queen?" Veronica joked, as she emerged into the living room of the suite.

"I think you look cute, like a teenager." He smiled.

"Wow, what did you put in that coffee?. Veronica screeched.

"I'll drive, I know the way," Brent said, changing the subject to one less embarrassing.

"Thanks, I'd rather just sit and veg

"Veg until your heart's content," Brent chuckled.

They pulled into the long narrow driveway, that led to Hillcrest Manor. Brent parked his truck in back of the house, near the garden path, and then they entered the house through the outside staircase, that led to each of the three levels of the house.

When they reached the two attic bedrooms, Veronica pulled the hidden staircase down, that was perched in the middle of the ceiling, behind the hallway staircase.

"Wow, I forgot how intricate, and huge this place is. Every landing has a window seat and stain–glass windows. You could film a real horror flick in here," Brent's jaw dropped.

Veronica's face flushed in embarrassment.

"Oh Veronica, I didn't mean anything by it. My mouth sometimes runs quicker than my brain," he squeezed her arm.

"You're probably right; I certainly can lend plenty of material to create a flick."

The closer they got to the top of the stairs, the dustier the place appeared to be. Anyone entering could tell the attic storage area suffered from years of neglect.

"Whew! It stinks in here," Veronica coughed.

"I'll open the window."

"It doesn't open, hasn't as far back as I recall."

Brent walked over to an area that was covered in blankets and old sheets.

"I think I see a fan in this mess." He peeled back a dusty, old sheet, and pulled out a floor fan.

"Yep, here it is!"

"How'd you find that?"

"I'm a cop, remember? It's my job to sniff things out; in this case, a fan."

Brent wiped off the dust, and then looked for an outlet. "Now we'll see if the thing works. Is there an outlet in here?"

"Yeah, I think it's by the window."

Brent walked over to the window. He moved several stacked boxes out of the way, until he got to the outlet, then he plugged in the fan. "Yes! We have air," he shouted.

Veronica had been rummaging through a group of boxes, and some plastic bags of clothing. "Now, if we could find this imaginary cedar chest."

Brent worked in the left–hand corner by the staircase. He

removed several boxes, and several old blankets and sheets that were sitting on top of an unidentifiable object. When he removed the last layer of blankets and sheets, he found a large, square object, covered by an old, wrinkled afghan. He removed the afghan, expelling the dust. Then he turned to Veronica, pointing to what appeared to be a trunk that had intricate carvings on the lid. "Could this be the cedar chest in question?"

Veronica walked over to Brent to discover a beat-up old trunk, then she glanced at the hand-painted flowers on its sides. "That must be it." She pulled at the brass lock, but it held fast.

"Great, it's locked," Veronica huffed.

"Hey, did you forget I'm a cop. I can pick this thing in a heartbeat."

Brent motioned for Veronica to stand back, while he worked on opening the lock, and then with one swift move, Brent released the lock.

Veronica clapped her raised hands, as if in a cheer, as she spoke. "Wow! I'm totally impressed. They did teach you something at that academy, after all."

"Well, Madam, it's all yours."

She stood there several minutes looking at the cedar chest, not moving or saying a word.

"Veronica, are you going to stare at it, or open it?"

"Yeah, I know. I'm getting my courage up. I'll look in it soon."

She moved closer to the chest, then looked at Brent, and said, "Here we go!"

She knelt down in front of it, and removed several envelopes from the chest, but nothing of importance was in them. She took a worn–down book from the chest, "*Gone with the Wind,* it was Mom's favorite book," she sighed.

A few more books of her mom's, and then some things of her dad's; a pair of leather gloves, a hammer, a pen knife, and then she found her christening dress. Tucked in a corner pocket, rested an envelope labeled, **Veronica.**

"I think I found it."

"Open it and see what it says."

Veronica caught her breath, "Not here, not now. I'll deal with it tonight alone."

Brent came over and patted her on the shoulder. "I understand; are you ready to go then?"

"Yeah, let's get out of here; I'm starting to get the creeps."

That night Veronica wrote this account in her journal;

> *The weather-beaten cedar chest stood in the forsaken, Victorian attic, covered with cobwebs and dust that collected over a lifetime of grief. I was afraid to lift the rusted lock that held the secrets to my family history.*
>
> *My friend spotted Mother's old coverlet, lying in the corner, crumpled up like a sad, old woman. Coffee stains and stale perfume filled the folds of the blanket. He exorcised the dust from it, and laid it down on the rotted, wood floor. So, it began: my staring contest with this evil chest, that held my family secrets. It seemed to take on a life of its own, daring me to expose its contents. This old cedar chest is the last piece to the puzzle of my mother's sad, manic life.*
>
> *The mere presence of that hideous chest, caused me to forget my fear, and now the desire to destroy its right to exist had emerged. I lifted its ancient lid with vengeance. Hidden memories of bloody family feuds, that led to the arrival of police, burst forth in my head, and with the onslaught of emotion rushing over my soul, the contents were exposed.*
>
> *Dust, mingled with my tears now created muddy streaks on my face. I was unaware of Brent's presence,*

although, I knew his hand was on my shoulder. It was a cleansing of evil, a release of soul. I sifted through the corroded papers and holiday cards, along with acid laden photos of people with lying smiles on their faces, a portrait of a family that existed only in the mind.

Then it appeared, sitting perched, and untouched by time like an evil entity. I couldn't open the envelope until this moment; an ivory colored letter, faded and wrinkled, hidden in my christening dress pocket, holding secrets it had no right to keep. The sorted words on the paper glared up at me, causing me to tremble.

Dear Veronica,

I'm leaving you with Uncle Jeb because I've failed you as a father. You need a stable life and Uncle Jeb can give you that. You're right about your mother; she does know what she is saying, and she doesn't care. I guess it has to do with the fact that your grandparents sent her away for help when she was young. Whatever the reason, you deserve to be loved, and so do I. Although I'm not sure God will grant me love, since I've failed you. I want you to know that I'm doing this because I love you, and I always will. I'm a beaten man, my lovely girl. I have nothing left to give you, except a better future with your uncle. Mom will be institutionalized for quite a while this time; maybe for good. May God forgive me, but I hope you get to grow up before she returns home.

With everlasting love,
Daddy

And so it happened. Mother was sent away by her family and Dad left her too. The poor, mentally fragile woman needed more than any of us was able to give. Dad needed his sanity, Grandpa and Grandma needed help, and I needed a chance at life. So what Dad did was an act of love, not abandonment, and from all indication, he still may be alive. Will I allow the cycle of rejection and abuse to continue in me? I'm a child of God now. He has healed my heart, and I trust He will take care of me. All I know is that I must find my father and tell him I forgive him, and that I will always love him too.

Then she sealed the journal shut.

What could drive Uncle Jeb to the point of lying about Dad? Veronica had always known him to be an honest man. Perhaps he thought he was protecting her from further hurt and pain, or maybe he couldn't bear to give her up. If she had known her father was alive, Veronica surely would have demanded to go after him; but then, it might have been the wish of a beaten man that her life be undisturbed.

How amazing it was to Veronica that one person's illness can ruin the lives of so many people. *Someday I will write a book about my experience. Others need to know they are not alone in their struggles. Little has been addressed regarding families of bipolar people; it's time their needs were addressed. Healing is not just for the sufferer, but for those who are the children, and the caregivers, as well, and as the good books says, 'with God all things are possible'."*

CHAPTER TWENTY-FOUR

When Veronica awoke the next day, she read the note again, and a wave of relief, mixed with sadness for the years spent hating her dad, came over her. Uncle Jeb unwittingly created a bad situation. She didn't fault him for it, knowing Uncle Jeb, his motive was pure love. The man hadn't a devious bone in his body. As she sat there contemplating her situation, the telephone rang.

Veronica answered it with a sullen tone of voice.

"Hi, it's Brent. Are you okay? You sound sad."

"I'm doing as best as can be expected. What's up?"

"I wanted to see how you were doing, and if you felt like going to lunch."

"I don't know if I feel up to it," her voice a mere whisper, as she struggled to get out the words.

"I'm sorry. This must be so hard for you, but I'm here to help; talking it over with someone, who cares and who is familiar with your family background can help to clarify things."

"I know that makes sense, but right now I'm tied up in knots. My emotions are going every which way. One minute I'm relieved to know the truth, and the next minute, everything breaks loose inside of me, and it doesn't help that I'm all alone here again, since Michelle took that little apartment behind the store where she works until I get the house in order."

"That's another reason why you need to be with a friend."

"I guess you're right. When Michelle was here, I worried about her, and didn't have time for anything else. Now that she's doing well, I have too much time to think."

"Veronica, somehow you'll get through this by finding closure, or a solution—either way, you'll need a friend."

"Brent, I think I want to find my father, to tell him I forgive him, and still love him," Veronica wiped a tear from her eye.

"I understand your feelings, but do you think that's wise? What if what you find, or who you find, is anything but what your memory holds."

"I'm sure it will be different. He will be different, I'm different; I get that, but for the sake of my peace of mind, I have to find out."

"Are you sure about this? Because if you are, let me come with you when you find him."

"I'm sure about it, and thank you for the offer, but I just need to meet him on my own." Veronica sobbed openly now. Tears flooded her cheeks blinding her vision.

"Veronica, I didn't mean to press you. I just thought you could use a friendly face out there on your own."

"I know, Brent, and I appreciate your concern, but I'm doing this alone."

"Then, I'm behind you one hundred percent."

"Thank you so much for that," she spoke as her voice cracked.

After sharing idle chit-chat back and forth, Veronica agreed to go to lunch. The mood was somber, but it did help her to put things into perspective. After lunch, Brent brought her back to the hotel room, making sure she was settled in.

"Well, I'll let you rest now; if you need me, just call." Brent touched her arm gently, and then he left her sitting on the sofa, where she stayed the entire night. She fell asleep to the eleven o'clock news, her robe wrapped around her ankles for warmth.

Somewhere between pitch black and dawn, Veronica heard strange sounds, like a child moaning. Then a young girl emerged in the corner of the room, crocodile tears cascading down her piercing, sapphire eyes. The child said, "I want my daddy," then she saw Uncle Jeb comforting the little girl and Veronica realized she was the child. Uncle Jeb seemed to be pleading with her, "Darling, I love you, and I won't ever go away." Then it dawned on her that Uncle Jeb drove the wedge between her and her father, probably out of fear that he'd lose his Veronica. As the years passed, and Veronica went off to college to study journalism, she gradually cut off all ties to her former life, including Uncle Jeb.

Somewhere buried inside was the knowledge that her father was still alive, but unable to face it, she buried herself in her work. Because of her obsession at finding what she believed to be the truth, she created a persona for herself that was less than loving; less than compassionate.

Veronica snapped out of this revelation. She touched her face, her skin was drenched with perspiration. *What did this dream all mean?* Veronica pondered how she struggled now to find God's truth and her true identity. It was ironic that the name *Veronica* translated into *true face,* was the opposite of what she had done all her life, by reporting a one-sided, bias version of a story, without considering all the facts.

To find a person's true face, or motive was not compatible with torturing people in pain and exposing their secret wounds for the entire world to scoff at. Somehow, seeing others suffer, evened the score for her. It was all very twisted and shameful.

Veronica thought about the day she and Michelle discussed the meaning of her name; she found it amusing. Now Veronica realized just how prophetic her name really was. Come to think of it, Michelle was the only person Veronica ever really had compassion for, at least after she had faced up to her original motives.

Veronica shook her body from head to toe, as if she could shake off the memory of this frightening revelation from her being. She checked the clock, and noticed it was 8:00 a.m. There wasn't any sense in going to bed, so she got up off the sofa, and went to take a shower. As she turned the water on to the bathroom shower, the telephone rang.

"Hello?" A sleepy Veronica yawned into the telephone.

"Hi, did I wake you up?" Michelle said.

"No, I was just going to take a shower."

"You sound exhausted."

"I didn't sleep much last night, but what's on your mind?"

"Well, I called to ask you if you wanted to go to church with me. The service is at ten this morning. I have been told the Pastor is a real compassionate soul."

"When did you get religion?"

"I think we both need it right about now, and your book did change my mind a bit."

"Oh, I'm so glad to hear that."

"Well, I want to try this and I need a little support. I think you need it too, so we can support each other," Michelle said.

"If you put it that way, I suppose it couldn't hurt," Veronica laughed.

"Good, come to my place around 9:45. Saint Michael the Archangel is just a block away from here."

"Oh, we're going to a Catholic church?

"Yes, I'm a baptized Catholic, I thought you were too."

"Yes I am. I guess that makes sense. Okay, see you then."

Veronica hung up the phone and headed for the shower. She was both apprehensive, and excited about going to church. She was a new Christian and up until now she had taken only baby steps in faith. She felt ill-prepared. However, since both of their families were Catholic, it made perfect sense to go to a Catholic Church.

She thought about Roy and how his Sunday worship was an expression of his Christianity, and she wanted that same thing for herself. Going today to a worship service with Michelle seemed right, felt comforting.

Veronica dressed in a pale grey pantsuit with pink shell and fitted jacket. She put on her black pumps and silver earrings, and then brushed her hair back into a bun at the nape of the neck.

She stepped back and looked at herself in the mirror. "This is good, I don't want to look too prudish, or too flashy; yes, this is just right."

Dressing on the conservative side was something new for her, and it was going to take a little more practice. Then she left and drove to Michelle's place.

Just as Michelle was putting on her shoes, the doorbell rang and she hurried to answer it.

"Hey, how are you?" Michelle's grin reached across her face.

"Boy, whatever Dr. Bookman has given you sure is working, could I have some?" Veronica laughed.

"Actually, I'm down to one antidepressant a day. I feel great. God is so good."

"Yeah, I'm still having a little trouble with that theory at times, especially when things are going poorly."

"I understand. I feel that way sometimes too. I think it's that way with everyone at times."

"I suppose you're right. After all, we're Christians, not robots," Veronica smirked.

"It's a fact that children from abuse have a harder time with the concept of a loving God, who cares for them unconditionally, no matter what they've done or will do, than those who have been nurtured properly from birth."

"You're starting to sound like Dr. Bookman."

"Well, she's given me lots of reading material."

"What else do you know, doctor?" Veronica rolled her eyes.

"You've been programmed to believe you're useless and not worth anything much at all. That kind of verbal abuse takes time to undo," Michelle squeezed Veronica's hand.

"Yeah, remember when we were kids and we'd say *sticks and stones will break my bones, but words will never hurt me?*"

"Yeah, I do. That is a false statement. Words damage a child much more, because they go straight to the heart and soul."

"That's for sure," Veronica's eyes grew wide.

"That's why I'm going to try hard never to take out my frustration on my little son."

"My dad used to say, it's better to count to ten first before you say something you'll regret. I only remember him losing his temper with me once. I was about six years old and we were in a candy store. I wanted bubble gum, but he said no because it would ruin my teeth. Well, I carried on something awful and he yelled at me, there in the store. He apologized later, saying that he shouldn't have lost his temper, but I was still being grounded for a week; no television, no friends."

"Wow, he sounds like a real decent man and that's some good advice," Michelle smiled.

Veronica and Michelle walked down the street to the church and entered through the main entrance, sitting in the middle of the church, in close view of the altar.

"Is this okay for seats?" Michelle touched her arm.

"Yes, it's fine, but how did you know I didn't want to sit up front?"

"Because I'm nervous too, and didn't want to sit up front on my first visit."

"You know, you're very perceptive."

The choir began to sing "Amazing Grace." The words filled Veronica's soul, and gave her peace. Then the Pastor entered from the back of the church and approached the altar. As Veronica sat there, listening to the prayers and chants, blessings and readings; she recalled her time at Uncle Jeb's when they had attended a Catholic church just like this one. Those were sweet memories. Uncle Jeb, she, and Millie had always gone out for breakfast afterward.

Then Father Jacob stepped up to the podium. "Good morning everyone, I'd like to read from Matthew 23:37 "Oh, Jerusalem, Jerusalem, you who kill the prophets and stone those who hurt you, how often I have longed to gather your children together, as a hen gathers her chicks under her wings, but you were not willing."

"How many times has Jesus come to you wanting to hold you and protect you? Yes, even heal you and deliver you from your self-destructive behavior. You say, 'I don't have self-destructive problems.' We all do, my people. Maybe you starve yourself to look good because you have a poor self-image, or you're a workaholic because you can't deal with your life, working gives you importance. My people, your self-worth comes from God. You're of great importance to Him. Remember He said you're worth more than many sparrows."

"Now, let us pray. Father, may each and every person in this church today feel the healing power of your love. Transform them Lord, so that they will see themselves through your eyes. Break destructive behaviors, and replace them with the fire of the Holy Spirit. In Jesus's name we pray."

Veronica and Michelle left the church. They walked back to Michelle's place in silence, when they reached the apartment. Veronica broke the silence. "Wow! That was some sermon. You know, I remember going to church with my Uncle and his girlfriend, but I never remember any sermon like that one. Usually the priest just reiterated the gospel with a comment about it. I remember being bored."

"The church has come a long way, and also, I told you that I heard he was good—a real motivator," Michelle smiled.

"It really hit home. I see the church in a different light now. Thanks for inviting me."

"You're very welcome. Shall we go to Hillcrest now?"

"Sure, let's go." Veronica said.

Veronica drove up the long driveway that led to Hillcrest Manor, the Hudson River served as the backdrop.

"Well, here we are, Psycho Hill, ah, I mean Hillcrest Manor," Veronica quipped.

"Well, it isn't Psycho Hill anymore, Veronica."

"I know, not as long as you and your son are here."

"It's funny; you always say me and my son with such conviction."

"That's because I really believe it will happen for you. Look how far you've come; from cashier at the deli, to Bank Teller, and living on your own; that's a lot of progress!"

"I know, and I do believe I will get him back too. I'm so sure of it, that I started looking for baby furniture."

"Michelle, I know there's some stuff in the attic, maybe you could use it for now."

"That would be great!"

They walked into the house from the back entrance, which faced the riverbank. In front of the basement door lay a small brick—paved area that would serve as a patio.

"This is charming; I could sit here and watch the Hudson River boats with my baby."

"Yeah, it's peaceful here early in the day."

Veronica opened the door and ushered Michelle inside.

"Oh, I love the hardwood floors."

"Yeah, these are the originals too."

"Are the leather loveseat and sofa staying?"

"All the furniture is staying, and that's a real working fireplace." Veronica pointed to a stone fireplace against the back wall.

"Oh that's really nice!"

Veronica opened the double doors on the opposite wall of the fireplace. "Let me show you the bedroom. Its small, but there's enough room for the crib."

"I love the rattan furniture, nice for a kid's room."

"Yeah, it will work just fine. Let's go into the kitchen." Veronica walked ahead, with Michelle following right behind.

"It's a small working kitchen with only that tiny table and two chairs against the window, but it has all you need. What do you think?"

"I think it's just perfect," Michelle grinned from ear to ear.

"I think the bedroom is large enough to fit in a crib and changing table."

"I think so too. I'm so glad you like it. Shall we check the attic for baby things?"

"Sure, let's go!"

Veronica led Michelle to the first level of the house, then the second, and third, until they reached the attic stairs. All the way up, Michelle looked around, eyes bugged out and mouth hanging, as if she was in a museum.

"Your family wasn't exactly poor, were they?"

"My mom's father owned a lucrative recycling business. He left this house to Uncle Jeb, and his stocks to Mom, but mom's medical needs ate most of that up, so we were the poor relations."

"That's too bad."

"Yeah, what can you do?"

"This house is yours now, so that's good."

"Exceedingly good, I'd say," Veronica laughed. "Here we are, the Hillcrest Manor secret attic," she smirked.

They rummaged around, finding a small hand-painted crib, a box filled with baby clothes, and some coverlets.

"Was this stuff yours?"

"No, I think it was Uncle Jeb's daughter's things. She died as an infant."

"Oh how sad."

Michelle's eye caught sight of the cedar chest. "This is gorgeous," she said.

"That's the infamous cedar chest, but it's all beat up."

"This can be restored. The lines and cut-outs are so intricate."

Michelle ran her hands over the surface, feeling every crevice and nook.

As Veronica watched Michelle admiring the cedar chest, she got a brilliant idea, it would be nice to restore the chest for Michelle, as a housewarming gift, and she made a mental note to find a refinisher.

"When can I move in?"

"I need to get some stuff in order first, but I think next month will work out."

"Great!" Michelle shouted out.

"Welcome to Hillcrest Manor, Ms. Martin!" Veronica shook her hand. "I'm sure you'll love it here."

"I know I will, and by the grace of God...so will Ryan!"

CHAPTER TWENTY-FIVE

It was late afternoon when Veronica returned to the hotel. She was emotionally and physically exhausted, to the point of collapsing on the bed, fully dressed. She kicked her shoes off, pulled the blanket over her body, then fell asleep, hugging the pillow.

She was awakened by the telephone ring. Somewhat groggy and confused, she caught a glimpse of the time on the alarm clock, and as she reached for the telephone, it occurred to her that she had slept several hours. She picked up the receiver, and glanced out of the window to witness the sun setting over the Hudson River.

She rubbed the sleep from her eyes, as she answered the telephone."Hu– Hello?" She cleared her throat.

"You sound sleepy, did I wake you?" Brent said.

"I must have dozed off when I came home earlier. What's up?"

"I think I found your father."

"wha– what? Where is he. Oh I just can't believe this is really happening," Veronica gasped.

"He's living in Florida."

"How'd you figure that, are you sure you have the right Wheaton?" Veronica's voice rang with suspicion; this news was too good to be true.

"Can I come over? It's hard to explain over the phone?"

"I, I sure—"

"I'll bring dinner; do you like Italian?"

"Yeah, I do."

"I'll be there within the hour."

"Okay, thanks Brent."

"Don't mention it."

Veronica hung up the phone, and headed for the shower. She allowed the cold water to massage her body, hoping the quick jolt of cold water would wake her up. It felt refreshing, like standing under a waterfall. As delightful as this experience was, she had to get ready, because Brent would be here shortly. Veronica dressed quickly, putting on a pair of blue jeans and sweatshirt. She was just about finished brushing her hair when the telephone rang again.

"Hello, Ms. Wheaton, this is the front desk. Sergeant Bishop is here to see you." The front desk attendant's voice sounded strained.

"It's okay, send him on up."

When Brent reached the hotel door, Veronica was waiting, wearing a smirk on her face.

"What are you grinning about?" he furrowed his brow.

"It's just that I sensed the front desk attendant thinks you're here to arrest me, or something."

Brent held up the bag of food. "Yeah, I always arrest a person with a bag of Italian food in my hand. That really breaks down a criminal, all the time," he laughed.

"Is that a new police tatic?" Veronica smirked.

"Yeah, I developed it myself. I call it the meatball affect."

"Ha, ha! You're so amusing."

"Thank you." Brent grinned. "I hope you like baked ziti," Then he placed the food on the table.

"I love it!" Veronica's eyes lit up.

"Good, because I got plenty."

"I love all pasta dishes. My Uncle Jeb used to say that I must have been switched at birth, and that I really belonged to an Italian family. For a while I truly believed him, until he showed me my birth certificate."

"With all you went through, he shouldn't have made such a crude joke," Brent squeezed her hand.

"I don't believe he meant any harm," Veronica said, as she reached for the plates and glasses.

Brent poured the wine and Veronica dished out the food, each having a large piece of Italian bread and a side salad.

"Mm, this is great ziti," Veronica licked her lips.

"Glad you like it."

"Now, let's talk about Dad," Veronica looked Brent in the eye.

Brent emptied the contents of the envelope onto the table.

"What's in this folder is basically all the records I found on your dad." He picked up what appeared to be hospital records.

"This folder is his medical history, right before he left you."

Veronica took the folder, little by little, scanning the pages, her expression void of emotion. Then she turned back to the page before, something there caught her eye. She gave it to Brent. "Wha what's this mean?"

"In a nutshell, the documents confirm that your dad was attacked."

"Attacked? How? But who did it?" she gasped for breath.

Silence fell for what appeared to be an eternity to Veronica.

"It's bad...isn't it?" she winced.

"Veronica, it says your dad tried to restrain your mom from thrusting a scissor into an aide's arm. It backfired, and he got it in the chest. It nearly killed him."

"How did she get a scissor? I thought patients weren't allowed to have sharp objects."

"They were at the nurses station, your mom ran out of her room. She grabbed the scissor from the nurse's counter."

"Oh I see, so why didn't mom get charged with assault?" Veronica's sapphire eyes pierced through Brent's heart, so much pain and anguish in her expression nearly caused him to lose control of his emotions.

"I understand that you'd want her to pay for her crime, but at the time it was determined as self-defense, since your father tried to put her in the hospital against her will."

"Yeah, and so later on they let her come home," Veronica said in a wounded tone of voice.

"Veronica, this stuff is going to be hard to take, but remember your purpose is to find your dad."

"Yeah, you're right, so tell me all of it."

"Your dad went into surgery, and barely survived. It was several weeks later when he was released. The next address for him was Lodi, New Jersey, where he lived until four years ago."

"Lodi, New Jersey? Who is in Lodi?"

"Apparently he opened a mechanic shop; I have reason to believe your uncle helped him."

"Well, that would explain why Uncle Jeb said he was dead; if I had known Dad was in New Jersey, I would have demanded to see him."

"Veronica, based on all the evidence found, I believe it was a mutual decision, in order to protect you and give you a stable home."

Veronica's eyes filled with tears, "But I needed him. He'd had to have known that!"

"I'm sure he had known, honey, but they did what they thought was best for you." Brent squeezed her hand.

"How'd you find out he was in Florida?"

"I have a buddy who works in the Tampa Police Department. I know your dad sold the mechanic shop at age 63, along with his house, so I just took a hunch that he would retire there, and I was right."

"This document says Tampa, Florida."

"Redington Beach, to be exact."

"Where is that?"

"It's about 25 miles west of Tampa. My buddy says it's a nice quaint community by the beach."

"Has he seen Dad?"

"Yes. It seems he owns a sightseeing cruise line. When he's not working, he can be found at the beach."

"Then, I guess I'm going to Florida," Veronica smirked.

"Honey, are you ready for this?"

"Yeah, I need to find him and hear his side of the story. I need my dad back; no matter what."

"Do you want me to come with you?"

"No, I need to do this alone."

"Well, let me give you the name and number of my buddy down there in case you need help."

"Thanks Brent, you have been a real friend."

Brent left Veronica the information, along with well wishes as he headed out of the door. For the next half hour she went over every scenario in her head. *What if my father doesn't want to see me? How would I cope with that? What if what he told me was so bad, I couldn't find a way to forgive him?*

She began to tremble from fear of what was ahead. So she did what had now been her stability since receiving Christ. She called Roy.

"Hello," Roy said sounding half asleep.

"Hi Roy, It's Veronica."

"What's up. Are you okay?"

"I'm sorry to call at this late hour, but I need prayer."

"Okay, do you want to talk about it first?"

"I found my dad. He is living in Florida."

"You did, so he's not dead after all."

"No, he's not, and I'm leaving tomorrow for Redington Beach, where he supposedly resides, to talk with him."

"Does he know you're coming?"

"No, that's why I need prayer."

"Don't you think if you called him, it would make it easier when you got there?"

"I can't handle that right now. I just need to get there."

"Okay then," Roy cleared his throat and began. "Dear Lord, Veronica needs your protection and strength right now. She's going to see her dad, and it may get ugly. No matter what happens, give her peace and wisdom to accept your will. Amen."

"Thanks, Roy; that was beautiful, and thanks for your support through all this."

"You're welcome and God bless you. Veronica, please be careful."

"I will be. I'm not expecting much, just some sort of explanation from him, no matter how lame."

"Just keep praying, as we will be praying here too."

"Bye, Roy."

CHAPTER TWENTY-SIX

Veronica boarded the plane at White Plains Airport, headed for Tampa, Florida. As the plane taxied down the runway, myriad of thoughts, most of them dark, and gloomy, danced across her mind. First, she saw her father as a young man playing with her on the living room floor of their old house. He was trying to distract her, while Doctor Lewis tended to her mother.

He was a friend of the family, who had treated Mom at home when she was unable to get to his office. Then the scene changed to the present, her dad, an old wrinkled up, expressionless man, standing like a corpse, as she yelled at him for abandoning her.

Veronica began to tremble at the thought of meeting her father face to face. In order to shake off this feeling, she ordered a drink, something she had not done in months. However, the smooth taste of the red wine lulled her into a state of calm.

After she finished the wine, Veronica closed her eyes, in an effort to catch a few moments of sleep before arriving in Florida. She fell sound asleep, and woke up when the pilot announced arrival at Tampa International Airport.

Veronica deplaned, grabbed her luggage, and then headed for the rental car counter.

"Can you tell me how to get to Redington Beach from here? She asked the young man at the car rental counter.

"Yes, I can," the young man pulled out a map and pointed to a spot. "Take a right out of this parking lot and make another right onto the Airport Road. Follow that over the Courtney Campbell Causeway. Stay straight, that road is now called 60 West, follow that for several miles, until you see a sign that says Clearwater Beaches. Then you need to follow those signs." The young man marked the route on the map, then handed it to Veronica.

"Thank you; have a nice day," Veronica said.

"Enjoy your trip," he smiled.

Veronica put her suitcase in the trunk of the silver Toyota Camry and then drove off, following with care, the mapped route.

As Veronica approached the Courtney Campbell Causeway, a bridge that hugged and stretched across Tampa Bay for almost ten miles, she marveled at the clear, crisp water that flowed underneath, it almost felt as if she was gliding on top of the water, and not the bridge expansion. In the distance, a group of boaters sailed on the blue waters, as seagulls and dolphins danced to the rhythm of the boats. She rolled down the windows, breathed in the invigorating fresh clean air from the bay, and it gave her a dose of courage for the mission ahead.

As she made her way to the Clearwater beaches, going over a second bridge, spanning another body of water, she took in the various beach shops and beach front hotels that combed the narrow thoroughfare. She checked her map, and realized this body of water was the Gulf of Mexico. Then she saw a sign that said 'Redington Beach city limits', so she pulled into a small motel to get a room. She parked the car by the side entrance, facing the pool, that gave a breathtaking view of the Gulf of Mexico. Veronica enjoyed the beautiful scenery; The sunshine sparkling on the water's ripples, before heading for her ground floor room to unpack.

The room was simple, but clean. There was one queen sized bed, a nightstand and TV cabinet. A table and chair set, suitable for two people, stood by the left side of the sliding glass doors that led to the patio.

Veronica spread Brent's research papers on the table and scanned through them, to find the address of the sightseeing boat company that her father owned; **Blue Dolphin Cruises, Dance with the Dolphins,** was the motto.

Veronica dialed the number on the piece of paper, half hoping no one would answer, but just as she was going to hang up, a voice said, "Blue Dolphin cruises, Ben Wheaton speaking."

Veronica froze in place when she heard her father's voice. *Was this real, could that truly be her dad on the other end?*

"Hello?" He kept saying, but Veronica couldn't speak, so she hung up the phone.

She sat down on the bed, and shivered for a good ten minutes before she was able to think clearly. Deep in the back of her mind somewhere, meeting her father was just an idea, but now it was real, too real to ignore.

She dialed the telephone again, but this time to Roy.

"Heritage World News, Roy speaking."

"Hi, Roy, it's Veronica."

"You sound upset. Did you meet your dad?"

"No, but I called his place of business."

"And what happened, did you talk with him?"

"He answered the phone, but when I heard his voice, I went cold inside and couldn't speak."

"Veronica, that's perfectly normal. Don't let that color your feelings about talking with him."

"I know you're right, but it's just so hard," she sniffled.

"I think you're too vulnerable right now. Wait until tomorrow; get a fresh perspective on things."

"Yeah, that's a good idea. I have the entire Gulf of Mexico before my eyes; I think I'll take a swim."

"That sounds great, take one for me, and then have a nice meal—and don't forget to pray for guidance."

"I won't, Roy. I tell you what; I can certainly understand why my dad came here. It's gorgeous on the Gulf."

"Well, you see, that's a start. You can empathize with him about the decision he made to move there."

"Thanks, Roy; you're the best."

Veronica hung up the phone and changed into her tank top and shorts, then headed for the beach. She spread her towel on the silky smooth sand and sat down. What amazed her was the fact that the sand didn't burn her feet when she walked on it, like the sand on the northern beaches did.

The warm Gulf winds caressed her face, and blew away her fears. Sunbathers passed by in a variety of beach wear. Young people, old people, families and teenagers of every shape and color; all enjoying together, and it gave Veronica a sense that things are not always bad in the world.

At the water's edge, two children made a sand castle and were waiting with excitement for the water to flow through their sand made moat.

Veronica walked down to the water's edge, and allowed the warm waters of the Gulf to tickle her feet. It was relaxing, as if the Gulf was giving her a foot massage. As she continued walking along the rim of the water, she thought about what she would say when she met her dad. She needed to keep her cool, not being judgmental, or argumentative. The best solution was to hear his side of the story before she answered him. *But could she do that?* She wasn't sure.

Suddenly, the water rippled under her feet. She stopped, allowing the tickling sensation of the waves, to fill her soul, as the sunrays danced across the water. In the near distance, a cruise boat was passing by. She squinted to read the logo on the boat, then she held her breath when she saw, **Blue Dolphin Cruises, Dance with the Dolphins.**

Time stood still, as Veronica acknowledged the fact that she was within feet of seeing her dad. She ran back to her blanket, shaking every inch of the way. When she got there, she picked up her things in one quick scoop, and walked off the beach. Back in her hotel room, she threw herself on the bed, wet, sandy feet and all, and just cried. *What will tomorrow bring? How am I going to pull this meeting off without falling apart? God please make this easier for me, if you will.*

Only time would tell what was in store for her. For now, time was all she had.

CHAPTER TWENTY-SEVEN

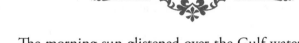

The morning sun glistened over the Gulf waters, and into her hotel room, ushering in a new day. Veronica opened the terrace door and stepped outside, drinking in the Gulf winds. Feeling refreshed, she ordered room service, and then jumped into the shower. She just finished dressing, when the bellhop brought her order of blueberry waffles, coffee and fruit salad.

She sat at the patio table, which faced the beach, to eat breakfast and watch the early risers taking their morning jog on the beach. *It must be wonderful to live in an environment where you can experience the beach every morning before work.* She basked in the warmth of the sun for a few minutes, and then said a silent prayer.

"If I'm going to do this thing, I had better get dressed and go. It's now or never!" She put on shorts and a tank top, then left the hotel. She made her way down Gulf Boulevard toward the Blue Dolphin Cruise pavilion, one mile down the road. As she drove passed condos and fancy hotels, she thought if she'd be as happy as the tourists on the streets after meeting her father.

She approached the roadway that led to the Blue Dolphin Cruise line; a small blue shack with a big blue dolphin on its roof; in front of the place were several parking spaces.

As Veronica approached the entrance of the pavilion, she noticed at least a dozen parked cars in front of the place. She pulled into one of the empty spots, and took a deep breath before heading for the front door. She opened the screen door that was reminiscent of an old country candy store door, and she smiled, remembering Uncle Jeb's old general store back home.

When she entered the lobby, she noticed a sizable group of people waiting on line for cruise tickets, excited tourists wearing their tropical gear, with fancy cameras hanging from their necks, wanting to capture memories. She listened in on two people, who were talking about the cruise, saying that this cruise was the best dolphin watching cruise in Clearwater Beach.

For a brief moment, she was proud that her father had done well for himself. Then he turned toward the customers. His eyes were shining and sincere, his hair, now salt and pepper in color.

She watched as he greeted his customers with a warm smile, answering their questions. He always was kind and gentle to everyone. Then it was her turn. He turned toward her and looked into her eyes. "Yes, can I…" He didn't finish the sentence, but stood transfixed, as he realized it was his child.

"Ron–, Veron…? Tears formed in his eyes.

"Yes, Dad, it's Veronica." Now tears filled her eyes as well. Everything she'd planned to say somehow didn't matter anymore.

"I've prayed for this moment; I've wanted to go back so many times. I always cherished those photos of you growing up that Uncle Jeb sent to me. But I just…" Then he left the counter and rushed to hug her.

They hugged for what seemed like an eternity to Veronica, a sweet loving eternity, that she never wanted to break free from for the rest of her life. Suddenly, she was that little girl, happy to be in her father's arms, knowing all would be right with the world, but then she snapped back to the present, and realized he had left her and disengaged from his embrace.

Finally her dad broke the silence. "Let me cancel this cruise and close up so we can talk."

"No Dad, don't disappoint them, besides I'd like to take the cruise too," she smiled.

Ben wiped his eyes. "Okay then, let's go find the Dolphins."

They walked arm and arm onto the boat. Tourists waited patiently for the cruise to begin. Ben took hold of the microphone and said, "I'm sorry, folks, for the delay, but this beautiful young lady is my daughter, and I haven't seen her in years."

Then someone shouted out, "Your daughter's Veronica Wheaton?"

Ben looked confused and said, "Yes she is, do you know her?"

Veronica pulled him close and whispered, "Dad, I'm a top reporter back in Rhode Island for the Heritage World News."

"Really?" he smiled.

"Yeah, we'll talk later about it."

Ben beamed from ear to ear, as he guided the boat to the dolphin's playground in the Gulf. Veronica listened as her father explained the nature and beauty of the dolphin. He was funny, as well as interesting, as he answered his customers' questions. He seemed truly at home in his field.

When the boat finally docked, it was early afternoon and Ben closed up for the remainder of the day.

"Why don't you come back to my place? It's only a short drive from here."

"Okay, if you're sure it's no problem."

"Not at all. You can follow me there, or we can pick up your car later."

"I would rather follow you there," Veronica answered.

They set off down the main road that hugged the Gulf of Mexico, along the way fancy hotels, bungalows and private beach homes aligned the shoreline. Ben turned down a sandy beach corridor, and then made a left turn into a small driveway. A blue and white beach cottage stood in front of her. In the back of the house was a tiny boat slip, that faced the inter-coastal waterway.

"This is a nice little cottage."

"Yes, we like it."

"We?" Veronica looked surprised.

"I remarried after your mother died."

"Oh, I see," she stiffened up.

"But I never stopped thinking of you...never!"

"We'll talk Dad, but not now. I'll be here until tomorrow afternoon." Veronica turned to leave; she couldn't handle the news of a stepmother, and was afraid she'd say something she would regret, but as she tried to leave, a woman with silver gray hair and blue eyes, opened the front door.

Veronica looked at the woman's warm smile, then back at her father's pleading eyes, and didn't have the heart to walk away now.

"Betsy, this is my daughter Veronica," Ben gave Veronica a look that said *please understand me.*

Veronica collected herself, taking a deep breath, then extending her hand for a handshake, "Hello, it's a pleasure to meet you."

"Well, it's a pleasure to finally meet you, dear, come in; you're more than welcome here."

Veronica smiled and entered their home. The place was warm and friendly, as if the people living in it loved life, and loved each other. Then it occurred to her, that her father deserved such a peaceful home, where Veronica had wished she'd grown up in with her dad.

Betsy ushered them into the patio that overlooked the boat slip. "I'll get some refreshments." Then she gave Veronica a hug and said, "I want you to know that he never stopped loving you."

Tears formed in Veronica's eyes, as her father looked on, waiting for the right moment to share his heart.

"Veronica, please let me tell you my side of the story."

"Okay, Dad, I'm listening," she touched his arm.

Ben took a deep breath, while he played with the buttons on his shirt, then he began. "When I left you with Uncle Jeb, I didn't know then that it would be forever."

"What happened? I know you were attacked."

"Yes, I went back to the hospital. Your mother was having a raging fit, I tried to subdue her, as apparently one of the nurses told her that I signed the papers to keep her in the facility long term, until she was totally stable."

"Where were the nurses? They knew she was unstable," Veronica's eyes watered.

"Your mother ran from her room just as I arrived. The nurses tried to stop her. I wanted to help. I thought if I could explain to her that she needed to be there for help, and I did it out of love; she'd calm down. However, your mother wanted to hurt me, because she believed I was conspiring with the doctors against her, and that I poisoned you against her.

"But that's stupid. She did that herself with all her bullying and verbal abuse."

"I know, honey. But she couldn't think things through like a normal person."

"So she stabbed you with a scissor? But the hospital records showed you almost died."

"Yes, I almost did. When she stabbed me in the chest, I fell against the counter hitting my head on a sharp object before plummeting to the floor."

"Okay, so after you recovered why didn't you come back for me?" Veronica's voice cracked as she spoke.

Ben reached across the table and took her hand.

"The stab wound hadn't been deep, but the blow to my head had caused me to be somewhat unsteady. Uncle Jeb had felt it wasn't good for you to have two unstable parents."

"What do you mean by, unsteady?"

"The blows to my head damaged my memory, as well as my reasoning skills. In short, I'd forget where I was and then I'd get angry."

"Oh, so you came to Florida?" Veronica said, in a sarcastic tone of voice.

"No, Uncle Jeb found a rehab center in New Jersey, so he made arrangements for me. I was too out of it to fight back."

"So Uncle Jeb took you from me?" Veronica's eyes narrowed.

"No, honey; he did it out of love. He never meant to hurt any of us."

"How long were you in rehab?"

"About three years. One year in residence, two years as an outpatient." Ben sighed before continuing, "That's when I met Betsy. She was my outpatient social worker."

"Quite a love story," Veronica crossed her arms.

"No, it hadn't been like that. We'd been friends first before I asked her out," Ben's voice shook, as he tried to gain Veronica's acceptance, then he continued, "As crazy as this sounds, I still loved your mother."

"I know you loved her, but you do deserve better, and Betsy seems to be what you need. It's just hard to take it all in. After all, I'm your daughter. I needed you too," Veronica's tears flowed with ease now.

"I had wanted to find you, but then your mom came back to live at your house, and I didn't want bad things to happen again," Ben struggled to explain. He placed one hand over the over to keep them from shaking.

"How'd you know I was okay?"

"Uncle Jeb wrote to me. He told me you were doing well."

"I don't understand why Uncle Jeb kept it a secret, even after I was on my own; that doesn't make sense. I had a right to know!" Veronica's voice raised an octave, as she tried to make her father understand what she had suffered, not knowing where he was, or if he still was alive.

"I think he was afraid that if you found out, he would lose you, and he couldn't deal with that. I, on the other hand, had so much guilt, I couldn't think straight about the issue."

"But you got married. You didn't seem to have any guilt over making that decision." Veronica waved her hand in dismissal, and then said, "I guess I'll never understand all of this, but for my own sake, I'm not going to try. So, when did you marry Betsy?"

"Seven years ago. I wanted to find you, but I couldn't bring myself to go back there. For what it's worth, Betsy kept trying to get me to find you. She was in your corner. I'm so sorry, baby, for everything." Ben buried his head and cried. Veronica went to his side and hugged him.

"Dad, I forgive you, and it's good to know you have an honest woman by your side now. On another note, I'm different, now, I've gone back to my Catholic roots after a sort of spiritual awakening, I guess you could say. I'm not going to tell you that I'm okay with everything, but I'm going to try to bury the past as best I can…with God's help."

"Can we be friends? I don't expect you to want me to be your dad again."

"We can be friends, as well as father and daughter, again too. Nonetheless, I'll need time to sort things out. Please don't expect too much at first. I have a lot of healing to do."

"I know honey, but I'm so glad you're back in my life again, and I promise to be patient, because you're worth waiting for."

The moment was broken by Betsy entering the patio with drinks and chips. "So, are you two okay now?"

Ben got up and hugged his wife. "We're more than okay."

"Good, then let's fire up the grill and cook some burgers," Betsy's smile was warm and inviting, as Veronica patted her on the back, "thank you for encouraging my dad to find me."

"Don't mention it, honey."

Veronica helped her father, while Betsy set the table. When the burgers were ready, Betsy brought out some baked beans and a salad, and they all sat around the picnic table that gave a clear view of the inter-coastal waterway. They spoke of Veronica's job and her future plans.

"Well, I did work for Heritage World News."

"What are you doing now, then?"

"It's a long story, Dad. I think I may move back to Hillcrest Manor."

Ben looked reflective. "Why would you move back?"

"Amazingly, I truly love the place."

"Well, I'm glad to hear that. Will you work for the news in Tarrytown?"

"No, I don't think so. I think I need a change. I just haven't figured out what that change will be yet."

Then she turned to Betsy and said, "Thank you for taking such good care of my dad; now I can go home, knowing he is loved."

"You're welcome, honey, but your father is very easy to love." She paused and then asked, "will we see you again soon?"

"I'm sure you will, sometime in the near future."

"Take your time, honey. I understand you have a lot to sort out."

"Thanks for understanding."

"You must know you're a part of our family; always have been in our hearts." Betsy then went over to Veronica and gave her a hug.

"Well, maybe the next time you and Dad could come to see me."

"That sounds wonderful!" Ben's eyes beamed with love.

"I think I'll be going now. I have a lot to do before my flight tomorrow afternoon. Thanks for the dinner." Veronica got up from the table, her dad following her.

"Honey, can't you stay the night? It's been so long."

"Yes, we'd love to have you."

"Thank you both, but I must get back to the hotel and pack. Besides, I also need to make a few telephone calls."

They walked Veronica to her car, and then her dad hugged her as he said, "I'll miss you, Veronica. Please keep in touch."

"I will Dad, I promise, I will." Veronica hugged Betsy, then drove off down Gulf Boulevard toward her hotel. As she drove away, she thought of what her future might bring.

Is this the beginning of a happy family, or the beginning of a long line of secrets, still to be uncovered? Maybe God is smiling on me now; maybe I'll have the family life I've always hoped, dreamed, and longed for; maybe this time it will be possible. She hoped and prayed that there weren't any other skeletons in that cedar chest.

CHAPTER TWENTY-EIGHT

When Veronica reached her room, she changed into a pair of shorts, before heading barefoot down to the beach. She walked along the water's edge until she found a cool, soft sand spot to rest, while allowing the grains of sand to tickle her toes. Veronica embraced the serenity of the shimmering rays of twilight, that danced over the Gulf of Mexico.

What was she to do about the rest of her life? She no longer felt connected to her home, and work in Rhode Island. Despite the fact visiting her dad felt natural, she never liked hot weather year-round, and she could never go back to being daddy's little girl, even though their relationship was on the mend.

On the other hand, surely, she could see her father as often as she liked, since Florida was only a short plane ride away. To top things off, there was Hillcrest Manor, as well as Brent and Michelle, waiting for her to make a decision and become part of their lives. Veronica was in awe by feeling wanted by so many people. If anyone had told her this would happen a year ago, she would have laughed in their face. Did it have to do with her Christianity, or was it just a happy coincidence? She probably would never know for sure, or at least not now, time will reveal what had happened.

Although she missed Hillcrest Manor, her friends, and her newly discovered life, was it enough to keep her there? She worked hard to advance and develop a solid reputation in the Journalism field, and now she was considering calling it quits. Was she truly ready to accept the consequences of such a decision? The newspaper world would surely see her resignation as a defeat, a fall from grace.

But somehow, that wasn't a real factor in her decision making. Tomorrow she was going back to Tarrytown, New York before reporting back to work at Heritage World News in Newport, Rhode Island. After her successful assignment in Tarrytown, Mark decided to give her a second chance at her old job. She needed to figure things out sooner than later, and make a wise decision. She felt ill-prepared for it.

What if she made the wrong choice? Veronica made her way back to her hotel room, with the moon shining on her path. She felt emotionally and physically exhausted, but needed to pack. Just as she was about to lock her packed suitcase, the hotel telephone rang.

"Who could this be?" She picked up the receiver, "Hello?"

"Hi, Veronica, it's Brent."

"Hey, what's going on? Is something wrong, since I'll see you tomorrow?"

"No, not at all, I just thought you would like a ride home from the airport tomorrow."

"Oh, that's nice, but I'm taking the airport shuttle."

"Veronica, please let me pick you up."

"What's wrong, Brent?" Veronica felt her body shake in fear.

"Nothing is wrong, I just—"

"You just what?" she pressed.

"Veronica, Michelle's case came up this past week."

"So, what happened?"

"Well, it's not bad, but it's not good either."

"What are you talking about?" Veronica's voice cracked, as she spoke.

"Well, the judge says he wants to see her with the baby. He's ordering supervised visitation, and he will re-evaluate in two months."

"So, that's not an unusual decision. How is she with that?"

"She's a little bummed out, but she is willing to do anything to get her child."

"This is just a bump in the road. I know she can make it work for her."

"Yeah, I suppose so."

"Brent, what is the real reason you want to pick me up tomorrow."

"I miss you," he sighed.

"I miss you too, but I'm still not ready to make a commitment."

"I know, I know, but if I said I wanted to come for you because I missed you, what would you have said?"

"No!" she chuckled.

"And that's precisely my point."

"Okay then, you can pick me up at White Plains Airport. My flight comes in at 4:35 P.M. on North Air."

"Thanks, Veronica. I'll see you then, and have a good flight."

"Good night, Brent."

Veronica smiled at the thought that Brent missed her. Most guys she had known couldn't wait for her to go away. Now here was this guy, who wanted her around. What a strange, wonderful, and frightening turn of events these last few weeks turned out to be. First off, she almost loses her job, and then gets assigned to Michele's case.

As if that wasn't enough, she runs into Brent and rekindles their friendship, and to top it off, she reconnects with her dad again. Last, but not least, she becomes a Christian. All of it was very exhausting.

Veronica got into bed and dreamed of better days, filled with good friends, and possibly, a new job; aside from her fear, the idea was quite appealing. Then she pondered her life as part of a loving family, and this time the possibility of it that happening was very plausible.

The next morning, Veronica took one last walk on the beach, as the sun rose in the sky. It was breathtaking and powerful the way that different shades of light cast its rays on the water. Veronica felt they looked like tiny diamonds that danced and sparkled on the water's ripples. It seemed so amazing to her that every day the sun rose and set in such perfect order, since the beginning of time. She wished everything in life was that reliable and perfect. She took one last gaze on the sparkling water, then headed for her room. She ordered room service; a cup of coffee and a bagel, and then she headed for the shower.

She finished her breakfast, and made some phone calls to her boss and Roy. Then she sat and read the paper. Time passed in a flash, and she dressed for her flight home. Just as she finished putting on her makeup, a knock came at the door. Veronica went to open it, and to her surprise, found her father and Betsy on the other side.

"Surprise!" they shouted out to her.

"Wha, what are you doing here?"

"We wanted to see you off, honey."

"So we thought we would ride to the airport with you, so we could spend some time together," Betsy added.

"But, Dad I have a rental."

"I know that, but Betsy can follow in our car."

"That is so sweet and all, but it's not necessary."

"Honey, we want to do it," Ben squeezed her arm.

"Well, alright then. Dad, will you take my bags?" Veronica said, as she grabbed her purse. During the forty-five minute ride to Tampa International Airport, she and Ben talked about their lives; the different paths they took, and how even though the roads they travelled were miles apart, those same roads served to bring them together again. As they pondered life, Ben lightened the mood by asking about her career.

"So, you're a reporter; what prompted that type of work?" Ben said.

"I don't know really. Sometime in high school, I decided to go into journalism. I was always good in English. My nickname was 'stone-hearted Wheaton' at Heritage," she blushed.

"So you must be some top-notch reporter with that name given you."

"No, dad I was a mean, angry woman. I was taking out all my pain on other people, using the media as a scapegoat."

"I can understand that. I'm sorry you suffered so much pain because of your upbringing," Ben turned his head away from Veronica, in embarrassment.

"Actually Uncle Jeb was wonderful to me. As a matter of fact, I used to think of Hillcrest Manor as my castle, and I was the princess, waiting for Prince Charming to sail up the Hudson, and rescue me; what a dreamer, huh?"

"I'm glad to hear you were well-cared for, and had somewhat of a normal childhood."

"As a matter of fact, Dad, I'm renting the apartment in Hillcrest Manor to a friend, like I told you yesterday. But just until I can decide if I want to go back for good."

"What about your job in Rhode Island?"

"I've burned too many bridges back there. I need to start out fresh."

"Well, I think we all need that at some time in our lives."

"Yeah, I guess we do," Veronica sighed.

They pulled into the airport rental lot; Veronica returned the car, while Ben and Betsy waited in the airport terminal.

Then they entered the airport. "It's still early, want to get a cup of coffee?" Ben asked.

"Sure, I see a place by that newsstand." Veronica responded.

"Whatever you decide to do, honey. You'll always have us." Ben squeezed her hand.

"I know I will, and thank you. Life will find a way."

"Yes, it will, sweetie." Betsy assured her.

They walked to the gate together.

"Well, this is goodbye for now," Veronica said as she hugged Betsy.

"We'll see you again soon," she assured her.

Ben approached Veronica and threw his arms around her, not wanting to let her go. "I'm going to miss you, baby."

"I will miss you too, but I'll call often," Veronica assured him.

"I would love that, baby." Ben watched his daughter walk away. His sadness at watching her leave, gave way to a sense of peace—this time, it would not be forever.

As the plane lifted off the ground, and Tampa became a speck on the ground, Veronica relived her visit with Dad and Betsy. She was happy for her dad. He finally had a good wife and a stable home life. She knew it will be impossible to erase the painful memory of the last several years; they would always be lurking in the back of her mind. However, now, she was strong enough to avoid the hurt.

When she exited the plane, Brent was waiting for her at the gate.

"Hey, how are you?"

"I'm good. I'm really good for the first time in a long time," she took a breath.

"That's great to hear," he squeezed her arm.

"Brent?"

"Yeah?"

"I think I'm going to give notice at Heritage World News and move back to Hillcrest Manor."

"That would be wonderful," his eyes lit up.

"You think so?"

"Yes I do." Brent's smile was warm and sincere.

"But I need a new job, and finding one in my field would be hard at best, given my reputation," she sighed.

"Well, maybe you should change careers?"

"Change into what?" she smirked.

"Maybe you could teach journalism, or English at the local high school. I know Mr. Pinkerton is retiring at the end of the semester."

"Really? Hmm... I wonder if I could do that. I mean, I hope I don't scare the kids half to death," she laughed.

"I'm sure you won't. They'll love you. If you want, I could ask the principal about it. He's a good friend of mine."

"I would love that. A good recommendation, especially from the police sergeant, could never hurt. Thank you. Brent."

"I'm sure with your background in journalism, there won't be a problem, especially since everyone loved your uncle."

"Yeah, I think I'm going to like living here this time around."

"I'm sure you will, too. You'll have me and Michelle to help you along the way."

"I know I do, and that will make it easier to handle the transition. It's time to make a real life for myself, one I can be proud of."

Brent pulled into the driveway at Hillcrest Manor. As Veronica entered the foyer, she looked around, and took a deep breath. She imagined herself living here, having a social life, and being very happy. Then she realized life didn't seem so bleak any longer.

CHAPTER TWENTY-NINE

Brent lugged her large suitcase up the old Mohangy staircase to her bedroom at the Manor. He tossed her suitcase on the four poster bed.

"Thanks, Brent. Want to stay for a cup of coffee?"

"No thanks, I have to get back to the station. I'll call you later."

"Okay, sounds good." With that Brent made his way down the stairs and out the front door.

Veronica unpacked, putting things away, and making piles of laundry. Then she checked the closet for linens. There, on the top shelf, was the old comforter that once adorned her bed; white with yellow and red embroidered roses. She loved that old comforter, the way that it kept her warm in the winter, and caressed her body when she felt all alone.

She took it off the shelf, along with the matching sheets. She sniffed the stale smell of the linens. "Looks like I'll have to do a wash." She sighed, then took the linens and headed for the first floor landing where the washer and dryer sat at the back of a long hallway that led to the back patio.

As she put the clothes in the wash, she noticed that Michelle was sitting on the back porch, looking at the boats that dotted the Hudson River. In one swift move, she opened the door and called out to her.

"Hey, Michelle, I'm home."

"Welcome home, Veronica. How did it go in Florida?"

"Come inside and I'll tell you all about it." Michelle reached the kitchen, just as Veronica was putting on a pot of coffee. Michelle sat down at the kitchen table, and motioned for Veronica to do the same.

"So dish, girl!" Michelle's eyes grew wide.

"Well, I spent two days with Dad and his new wife."

"His new wife?"

"Yes, and she's a wonderful person, just what my dad needed."

"And your dad, how is he?"

"He's just fine. He owns a sightseeing dolphin cruise business. Apparently, looking for dolphins in the Gulf of Mexico is big business," Veronica chuckled.

"So, you're okay with him, and he with you now?"

"Yeah, we are. It was rough at first, but he explained what happened and it made sense to me."

"Well, that's good news, Veronica."

"Yeah, it is," she sighed.

"You don't sound so sure about it," Michelle crinkled her nose.

"Well, it's a lot to take in. On one hand, I long to be close to him, like we were when I was young, and on the other, I fear he'll break my heart again. God knows I've been hurt enough," she said with a tone of sadness in her voice.

Michelle patted her arm. "I know you've been hurt a lot. I can understand how you feel. It's painful to trust people when they've betrayed you, but if his story made sense to you, well then...let it take its course."

"Yeah, I guess you're right. I'll just have to take it one day at a time."

"It will work out, but don't expect it to be easy. Trust yourself, just like you trusted your instincts about me."

"Yeah, that turned out to be quite a blessing for both of us."

"That's right, and now you have more going for you."

"How's that?"

"You have God to lean on."

"In other big news, I've decided to stay here at Hillcrest Manor. I don't feel that I belong in Rhode Island, or at Heritage World News any longer. I just don't have it in me to be that tough anymore."

"They say you're a new creation when you come to Christ. I guess with you, He worked really fast in changing your attitude. But that's not a bad thing. The next adventure will be just what you need, I'm sure."

"Wow, you're really positive lately, that's great! Anyway, I spoke to Brent, and he's going to ask the high school principal about a job; apparently there is an opening. Now, what's going on with you?" Veronica asked.

"That sounds wonderful! Well, I guess Brent told you about the judge's decision."

"Yes, he did, but that's not unusual."

"I know. I was bummed out at first, but this way it will give me a chance to transition into motherhood."

"Yes, and prove you're a good provider, as well, to all the naysayers."

"Yeah, I've been doing well lately," Michelle got up from the table and turned to Veronica. "I'll leave you to rest; you seem like you need it." Then Michelle gave Veronica a hug and headed for the door. She turned around just before exiting and said, "I'm glad you're staying here, welcome home."

"Thanks, I'll talk to you later," Veronica called after her, as Michelle started down the stairs..

The next day Veronica left in the early morning hours. She was hoping to arrive in Newport by lunchtime, so she could talk with Mark about her decision. The weather was clear and the traffic was light on I-95, so she managed to arrive earlier than expected. Veronica passed in front of the Java Coffee Café, where her fellow reporters use to meet before work or brought their sources to get information for a news scoop.

She decided to go in and have a cup of coffee for old times' sake.

No one she knew had arrived yet at the Café, for which she was grateful. She really wanted to be alone to think.

This would be the last time she'd drink coffee in this place, a place where she'd talked to sources, and planned her attack on unsuspecting citizens, just to get a juicy story. The place didn't carry the old charm anymore. While she sipped her coffee, she placed a call to Roy. She had promised him she would call when she was near the office. Why she had to call him, she didn't know. However, she had vowed and she would keep that vow.

"Roy Gibbons, Weather Anchor."

"Hello, Roy it's Veronica."

"Well, how are you, honey?"

"I'm fine. I just stopped for a cup of coffee. I should be at the office in twenty minutes."

"Great, I can't wait to see you." Roy hung up and spoke to the staff. "Okay everybody, Veronica is going to be here in a few minutes, so let's get this party going."

Veronica pulled into the parking lot at the news station, and then took the elevator to her seventh floor office. When she got off the elevator, she was greeted by an assortment of colorful balloons, bagels and cream cheese and a group of smiling faces yelling SURPRISE!

Roy stepped forward along with Mark, and the men gave her a hug.

"Welcome back, Veronica," Roy gave her another big hug.

Then Mark squeezed her arm, and said, "Ms. Wheaton, are you ready for your next assignment?"

Veronica hesitated for a minute, then said, "Not until I have a bagel and smear."

Everyone laughed and Veronica took the opportunity to mingle in the crowd. Leonard and Louise approached her, as she took a bite of a whole wheat bagel.

"Welcome back, Veronica," they chanted at the same time.

"Thank you. I want to apologize to both of you for my behavior toward you in the past," then she gave each one a hug.

"It's a new day; things will get better for you," Louise's smile was sincere.

"Yeah, I believe they will," Veronica said, then she caught a glimpse of Mark going into his office, so she followed after him.

"So let's talk, Mark," she said as she reached for the chair.

"Sure, have a seat. I understand that young lady, Michelle Martin, is doing well."

"Yes, yes she is."

"How are you, Veronica?"

"I'm doing fine, Mark. Everything is just fine now."

"Well, I have a story lead for you that will—"

"Mark, before you continue, I must tell you, I've done a lot of soul searching while I was gone, and I decided I need to start over," Veronica swallowed hard.

"I agree, so you can rebuild your reputation into something positive and trustworthy."

"No, that's not what I meant."

"What then?" Mark furrowed his brow.

"I'm resigning. I'll give you my resignation in a letter by close of business today. I will stay for two weeks and if you need, I can stay to transition the new person into my slot." Veronica took a deep breath, as she waited for Mark's response.

Mark cleared his throat. "Oh, I see."

"Mark, I didn't plan for this to happen, but while I was in Tarrytown things happened. Call it divine providence if you will," she shrugged.

"Roy said you got religion," he responded in disgust.

"Look, Mark, you didn't like me the way I was and intended to fire me. Now that I'm different, and I want to leave on my own, you seem annoyed," Veronica's voice quivered as she spoke.

"That— that's just different."

"How so?" she shrugged.

"Well, it just is," he huffed.

Veronica walked over to his desk and sat on the edge of it, then looked him in the eye. "Mark, I don't expect you to understand. Roy gave me this book before I left, and at first, I ignored it. Then you were all over me for bad behavior, and there was Michelle Martin, who reminded me of my mother, and so I read the book out of curiosity, and it changed me."

"And now you're the poster child for every televangelist," Mark glared at her.

"No, Mark. I accepted Christ, then things changed; I changed. I started to right my bad behavior; that's why I wanted to help Michelle. Then I found out my dad was alive and I needed to find him."

"Your dad?"

"Yes, it's amazing. He's living in Florida. I visited him over the weekend and we're okay with each other now."

"Okay, I get it, but why do you need to leave here?" Mark looked wounded, and confused at once.

"I just don't feel the need to be a reporter anymore; as a matter of fact, I plan on teaching at the local high school in Tarrytown."

Mark sat back in his chair and sighed. "Well, I guess all those legends about headless horsemen got to you, because you've lost your head for sure."

"Mark, please; I need your blessing."

"Does Roy know about this?"

"No, he doesn't know a thing about it. Please, Mark, your blessing is important to me," Veronica squeezed his arm.

"Tell Jennie to come in here. I need to send out a message to the staff. I'll want you here for three weeks before I cut you lose, though."

"Bless you Mark. Bless you," Veronica hugged him, then left the room.

Roy was waiting for her as she exited Mark's office.

"So is everything squared away between you two?"

"Roy, we need to talk," Veronica looked him in the eye.

"What's wrong?"

"Nothing; let's go to the break room." Roy followed Veronica down the hallway, and into a small alcove off the break room's kitchen area.

"So what's the big mystery?" Roy said looking rather nervous.

"I've resigned from Heritage World News. I'm going back to Tarrytown to work as a teacher at the high school."

"A teacher? You got a job?"

"Well not yet, but a good friend has a connection for me."

"So you may not have a job?" he smiled.

"Roy, either way, I'm going to move. I don't belong here anymore, and I have you to thank for that."

"How do you figure that?" he shrugged.

"You introduced me to your Savior and now I'm not the same," she squeezed his hand.

"But did He tell you to quit your job?"

"Roy, I don't fit in anymore. Back in Tarrytown, I have friends. It's good now."

"You can't rewrite a bitter past. What is done, is done."

"I'm not trying to. I just realized I love Hillcrest Manor. Michelle Martin is my tenant and Brent Bishop is a good, reliable friend. I have what I need, including a new start with my dad. I will always love you, Roy. You're the reason life is so good now."

"No, Veronica, God is the reason your life is so good now." Then he hugged her. Roy saw the joy on Veronica's face and he knew he had to let her go. He embraced her, and said, "Go with God, honey."

"We will always be friends, Roy. I will never forget you," Veronica said through tear-stained eyes.

CHAPTER THIRTY

The solid Oak and Elm trees that stretched across Veronica's property, looked as if they had been barren and spent from the blustery winter winds, that ushered in a new season. Veronica could feel their pain, she felt spent, as well. Now she was in the town of her youth, living and working with people who knew her family legacy; the good and bad of it. Somehow it didn't matter anymore; not to them and not to her.

The job at Tarrytown Hollow High School turned out to be quite an experience for Veronica. At first, it felt as if she had made a mistake, leaving her prestigious journalism career behind. Nonetheless, after settling into the routine of teaching, she discovered that molding, and guiding the future journalist, was very rewarding, and she loved it. Most of them seemed unimpressed with her past celebrity fame, except for Ann Marie Lynch, who was too taken up with the image of Veronica Wheaton.

As much as Veronica tried, she could not convince Ann Marie that reporting news was more than being on a witch hunt. The sad part was that Ann Marie Lynch had great potential, but Veronica was hard pressed to convey that message.

Time would tell where Ann Marie's attitude leads her. As for now, prayer was Veronica's main weapon for her students and herself. The winter break had come, and Christmas was only three days away. Veronica's relationship with her father grew strong in trust, so much so, that she invited Dad and Betsy to spend Christmas at Hillcrest Manor with her, as well as Michelle and Brent.

As the days grew closer to Christmas Eve, Veronica planned the menu, and took the decorations down from the attic. She unwrapped ornaments from her childhood, when she lived with Uncle Jeb. She came across some hand painted glass ornaments. Veronica recalled how much fun it was to paint Santa faces and angels together, with Millie on Christmas Eve. She recalled, back then she was determined to hurt everyone, and a tinge of remorse came over her.

Tucked away, in a large box, she found a colorful red box containing the gold beaded angel for the top of the tree. She and her father bought that topper together the Christmas before she came to live with Uncle Jeb. Veronica held it in her hands for a few minutes, remembering that special time, as tears of happiness rolled down her cheeks. She would save the angel for him to place on the top of the tree; a symbol of their newly found relationship.

Veronica snapped out of her daydream and got busy. Her dad and stepmother were coming Christmas Eve morning, and she had lots to do to prepare the Christmas turkey dinner, and get the house ready to decorate. Michelle volunteered to help with all the preparations, but Veronica didn't want to impose. She'd won her case in the court, and Michelle was now the proud mother of her fifteen-month-old baby boy, and she had her hands full learning to be a mother. But Michelle insisted, stating it wasn't imposition to help out her best friend.

As Veronica sifted through cookie recipes, she heard a knock at the front door. She put down the recipes and went to the door to open it.

"You don't have to knock when you come upstairs from your place today, the door is open."

"Well, I wasn't sure if you'd be in the shower, or something. Anyway, Ryan and I are here to help make the Christmas cookies," Michelle's warm smile lit up the foyer.

"That's very nice of you, and you too, Ryan." The baby laughed, as Veronica tickled his tummy.

"So, I have this recipe from my grandmother I thought you might like; it's for gingerbread."

"Sounds like fun, and I have an old recipe too."

"Your grandmother's recipe?"

"No, Millie's, my Uncle Jeb's girlfriend. She used to bake the greatest cream cheese cookies with cinnamon topping.

"Okay, so let's get started," Michelle said, as she placed the ingredients to make the gingerbread on the table.

Veronica gave Baby Ryan a wooden spoon, and he cooed and laughed around the kitchen table, as he waved it in the air.

"He's getting so big and adorable!" Veronica smiled.

"Yeah, it's amazing how fast they grow," Michelle kissed Ryan on the head, as he waddled by.

Veronica looked pensive. "What's bothering you. It's not the baby in the kitchen, is it?"

"Well, yes and no. I'm thinking about if I'll ever have a family, and I'm also worried about my father and Betsy coming for the first time."

"I'm sure you will have a family, you're still young, and as for your father; just wait until he tastes the cookies we make, why he'll be crazy about you all over again!"

Veronica smiled, "Yeah, I'm sure that'll do it."

Then Michelle squeezed her arm, "I know this has to be very hard for you, but I'm sure it will work out. I don't believe that God would put you two together again just to split you apart."

"Yeah, I guess you're right about that," she smiled.

"It stirs up dirt, right? That's what is really bothering you."

"Yeah, lots of dirt, but we did discuss a lot of this when I was in Florida. Sometimes, it's hard getting past it." Veronica wiped a tear from her eye.

"I know how you feel. I look at Ryan, and see his father in him. It's hard to let go, but you know what someone once told me?"

"No, what did someone once tell you?"Veronica grinned.

"That those things can't hurt you now, they only serve as a reminder that God is faithful, and He brought you out of your pain."

"That's good advice."

"Yes it is.I think we had better make these cookies before your family arrives, don't you?," Michelle smiled.

"So let's do it!" Veronica brought the rest of ingredients to the table.

The afternoon went by in a wisp on the winter wind. A few snow flurries began to fall, creating a white powder over the cars and sidewalks.

"I'm going to go down to my apartment to put Ryan down for his nap."

"You could put him in my room. We put those baby bumpers in my closet. Remember? For when I babysit him."

"I'll come back later on. I want to take a shower while he's sleeping."

"Sure, I'll see you later."

Michelle went down the back stairs by the kitchen with Ryan in her arms, the child was already asleep. Veronica packed the cookies in tins, and then sat down to relax with a few cookies and a cup of tea.

She thought about her life now, and all the wonderful people in it; Michelle and Brent, and the kids at school, and her dad and stepmother, and Roy from Heritage Worlds News. He remained true to their friendship and was always there when Veronica needed encouragement.

Veronica walked into the den and dusted the cedar chest off. Brent had brought it down from the attic for her, so she could refinish it for Michelle. She thought of sending it out to a professional refinisher, but after polishing the wood, she realized she could put her own personal touch to it.

The wood was a deep cedar with cut-out grooves along the edges. Veronica brought a stencil of bunnies, and painted them on in colors of blue and yellow. She planned to give the chest to Michelle for Ryan's room. As she re-polished the piece, she recalled all the mystery shrouded over this chest.

How it caused her so much anxiety at the prospect of what it contained, and then when the mystery was unveiled, how Veronica fell apart at the truth of its contents. It was only a cedar chest, but it held the fragile lives of so many people. It had the power to bring pain, to hold secrets, and to heal a family's hurts. In the end, she hoped that the chest would be a source of joy for Michelle and her son.

Veronica stepped back and looked at her masterpiece. It was finished and complete with all it's beauty. It had weathered every storm, even years of neglect, and it survived rising more radiant than ever before. Veronica realized that's just how God works in a soul. *He is there refining a soul at every turn, good or bad, and in the end, if it holds fast, it will be a thing of great beauty for all to enjoy.*

Time was ticking by fast, and with Christmas Eve the next day, Veronica still had some more work to do on the house before company came, like washing the old China dishes, cups and saucers that were her grandmother's, and washing the old table cloth that had been embroidered by her mother and grandmother. These things had always been precious to her, in spite of her circumstances.

Now she was ready to share this most precious season with her new family, the one she believed God had planned for her from the beginning of time.

CHAPTER THIRTY-ONE

Veronica woke up to the sound of the alarm clock blaring in her ear. Although she had lots to do before her father and Betsy arrived, she hit the snooze button for another ten minutes. When it went off the second time, she took a hot, steamy shower for a good start to the day. As the water massaged her body, she reflected on the past few months, and all the changes that had taken place in her life.

She had gone from being a heartless reporter, to a warm, caring Journalism teacher; except when Joey Wilson and his motley crew, consisting of Evan Walker and Mike Stingle, tested her patience and ended in detention, when they least expected it.

She then went from orphan and unwanted, to having the family and friends she longed for all her life, and now cherished. As God continued working in leaps and bounds in her life, sometimes she had to stop just to catch her breath from all the fast changes occurring, in her lifestyle and attitude, and she was thankful.

When Roy first told her about Christ, and His merciful love, she'd thought he was delusional at best, but now she knew that everything Roy had told her was true. As she put on her robe and slippers, she whispered a *thank you* to God for giving Roy the grace to be relentless in his pursuit of her soul.

After Veronica finished drying her hair, she walked down the staircase and into the kitchen. She fixed herself a cup of coffee, glanced out of the kitchen window, and was delighted with the ballet-like dance of the light, falling snow flurries.

"A true white Christmas. I hope that doesn't delay Dad's flight." Veronica watched the snow falling gently to the ground.

"Well I better get things started, so I can relax a little before Dad and Betsy arrive. I need to baste the turkey and get the vegetables cut up, but first I better press the Christmas linens," Veronica sighed, "I want everything to go perfectly."

She proceeded to the dining room carrying the already pressed finely embroidered Christmas tablecloth, a family heirloom she found in the attic. She proudly put it on the dining room table, placing one napkin next to each place setting. Then she took out her China and stacked them on the table.

Everything looked beautiful, as if in a fairytale. It was the way Veronica had dreamed her life would be; fancy holiday dinners, warm friends and family, and now it was actually happening. She pinched herself to make sure it was real. She still couldn't wrap her mind around the fact she had a family. It was a lot to take in for a girl, who had never known real stability for any length of time in her life.

Her dad should be arriving around early afternoon, if the flight wasn't delayed. She figured she had plenty of time to clean and get their room ready. She wanted to have dinner around 6 p.m., followed by opening the presents and ending their festivity with dessert. She hoped everyone was willing to attend the midnight mass at St. Michael the Archangel on Chapel Hill. She promised herself she wouldn't push the idea, though. If no one was up to it, she would just go to mass in the morning.

When she looked at the clock again, it was 11:00 a.m. If Dad and Betsy were on time, they would be arriving in one short hour from the White Plains Airport, then just a short ride to the house.

Veronica hustled up the staircase and freshened up, changing into black silk pants and a red silk shirt. She pinned her hair up into a bun and placed Christmas wreath earrings in her ears. Just as she entered the living room, a knock came at the front door. Veronica rushed to open it.

"Hi Veronica. I'm here to help with the finishing touches," Michelle said, as she reached for Ryan, who was trying to go down the front steps. "Honestly, I need four pairs of eyes for this one," she laughed.

Michelle picked him up and brought him into the house.

"It's going to be wonderful having a baby for the holidays," Veronica took Ryan from Michelle, tickling his stomach. "You look so handsome in your green velvet pants."

The baby laughed and giggled, as she tickled him. Then she put him down and he waddled around, checking out everything in the room. The women walked into the dining room.

"I'll finish setting the table for you, Veronica."

"That will be great because I need to tend to the bird!"

"It smells wonderful!" Michelle shouted after her.

As Veronica basted the turkey, the doorbell rang. She called out to Michelle, "I'll get it!"

She rushed with flushed cheeks into the living room to answer the door. Her emotions ran roughshod between happy, excited, nervous, and frightened, and she had all to do to keep it together. She said a quick prayer for peace and surrender to God's will, and then she opened the door.

"Hi, Daddy! It's so good to see you again." Veronica gave her father and Betsy a hug, as they entered the living room.

"Good to see you again, honey."

"Thanks, Betsy."

"Did you order the snowflakes, Dad?"

"Nope, but do you remember when you were a little girl, how we would say a prayer at your bedside that it would snow Christmas Eve?"

"Yes, I do remember that."

Then Betsy entered the living room, all smiles, giving Veronica a big hug. "Honey, this is a lovely home that you have."

"Thanks, Betsy. I remodeled it some from the original. You know, paint instead of wallpaper, and I had the back wall to the kitchen taken out, so that it flows into the dining area."

"Well, it looks beautiful." Betsy's eyes lit up.

Just then Michelle entered the living room from the kitchen with Ryan in hand. When he saw Ben and Betsy, he let go of his mother's hand, and waddled over to Ben cooing and laughing.

"Well, who's this little fella?"

"Dad, Betsy, this is my friend and tenant Michelle. This is her son, Ryan." Ben bent down to be on Ryan's level and shook his hand, "It's a pleasure to meet you, sir."

Ryan answered in baby talk, and then laughed; everyone laughed along with him. Then Veronica gestured to the stairs.

"Let me get you guys situated in your room."

"This was Uncle Jeb's room, wasn't it?" Ben said.

"Yeah, I painted it and had the furniture refinished," Veronica said.

Betsy scanned the room, "It looks wonderful, as if it was a room in a B&B."

"Thanks, Betsy, I appreciate it."

"So, your friend Michelle hasn't a husband?" Ben asked.

"It's a long story. Remember, Dad, when I was in Florida I told you about a case I was working on?"

"Oh yes."

"Well, Michelle was my client. I was sent here to investigate a news scoop about her husband, and when the case went down, she lost her son and didn't have a place to live."

"What happened?" Betsy asked.

"Her husband claimed she was an incompetent mother."

"Was she?"

"No, he planned the entire affair; so when they ruled in her favor, she hadn't a place to live, so I told her she could live here."

"So you offered her the downstairs apartment," Ben answered.

"Yeah, I did."

"I'm so proud of you, Veronica. What a selfless thing to do," Ben's eyes teared up.

"To be honest, Dad, only six months ago I would have let her rot, but since I found Christ, I think differently."

"I know, it's great, isn't it?" Ben smiled.

"You mean you're a Christian?" Veronica's eyes bugged out.

"Your father has been for years," Betsy said.

"Then midnight mass tonight will be okay with you? I'm a Catholic. I thought since I was baptized as a Catholic, I owed it to my faith to find out about it, and I really like it."

"Oh we would love to go. Back home we go to mass at St. Luke's." they answered in unison.

"So, you're Catholic, too?"

"Ben is as you know, but I'm still attending the R.C.I.A. program."

"Oh that's wonderful! Well, I'll leave you two to settle in. Come downstairs when you're ready."

Veronica went downstairs into the kitchen to check on the meal. She found Michelle fussing over the turkey.

"Were you expecting the entire neighborhood to join us?," Michelle laughed.

Veronica put her hands on her hips, "Well, I never cooked for anyone before, as a matter of fact, I never really cooked for myself either."

"I'm just kidding; it's always good to have leftovers. You and your folks okay?"

Veronica held up a hand to silence Michelle. "I have something important to tell you."

"What?"

"They are Christians. Daddy is Catholic and Betsy is going through formation to prepare to be baptized in the church.Isn't that amazing?"

"It's absolutely wonderful! Michelle shouted.

As Ryan heard the noise coming from the kitchen, he waddled in, clapping his hands. Both women let out a belly laugh at his perfect timing.

The afternoon passed by, with laughter and stories from times past and hopes of what the future held for all of them. Now it was time for the Christmas feast to begin.

Veronica set everything down on the kitchen table, and called for everyone to be seated.

"Veronica, what's with the extra chair?" Betsy asked.

Just then the doorbell rang and Veronica rushed to answer it.

"Here's our lost dinner guest," she laughed.

Ben stood to greet the young man, who towered over him.

"Dad, I'd like to meet my friend, Brent Bishop."

"You mean, Brent 'football star' Bishop?"

"Yes, that would be me," he grinned.

Ben introduced Betsy. "This is my wife, Betsy."

"I'm glad to meet you, Brent," Betsy extended her hand.

"So, what have you been up to since high school?" Ben asked.

"I'm the Sergeant of the Tarrytown Police Force."

"Oh, good for you!"

"I hear you run a Dolphin sightseeing cruise down in Florida."

"Yeah, I love those creatures; they are so playful and it's a big hit with tourists."

Then Veronica went back to the kitchen to get the turkey, she came back into the room and set it down on the table. "Dad will you do the honors and carve the Turkey."

"Sure, honey. I would love to." Ben took the carving knife and began to cut into the bird.

"Everything looks wonderful, Veronica. Two kinds of potatoes, two kinds of vegetables, stuffing, cranberries...you must have been cooking all week!" Betsy quipped.

"Well, Michelle helped me."

Everyone ate their full. Ben gave Ryan the Turkey drumstick, and it was a show in itself to watch him chew on it. As the meal came to a close, Veronica announced presents were going to be distributed in the living room by the tree.

"Well, let's see what Santa got you, big boy," Betsy said, as she carried Ryan into the living room. The child opened several packages of clothing, some building blocks and a dump truck, which he immediately took possession of.

Gifts were exchanged and cookies and cider passed out. Then Veronica leaned over toward Brent and whispered.

"Come into the den with me."

"Sure!" Brent said aloud.

"Don't be silly," she laughed, then she turned to everyone and said, "We will be right back, I assure you."

"Can you help me carry the cedar chest into the living room?"

"Sure, I can."

They lifted the cedar chest, then walked slowly into the other room. The chest was unwrapped, except for a big bow on top.

"Merry Christmas, Michelle" Veronica shouted, as Brent placed the chest in front of her.

"But this is your family's cedar chest!"

"I know, but I refinished it for you. See, it says Ryan on the side, along with his date of birth."

"This is very generous of you, but I can't take this."

"Of course, you can. Open the lid, Michelle, please!"

Michelle pulled out the card, then read it aloud.

Dear Michelle,

> *This cedar chest has brought pain, mystery, sorrow, tears and even joy to my family. Now that the legacy of the cedar chest is finished for the Wheaton family. My prayer is that for you and Ryan, it will bring nothing, but peace, joy and the full favor of God on your lives.*

Merry Christmas,
Veronica

Michelle put down the card and hugged Veronica, as tears streamed down her face.

"Veronica if it wasn't for you, I don't know where I'd be."

Veronica put her arms around Michelle's trembling body. "We are all links in a chain, Michelle. If Roy hadn't led me to Christ, I would not have had the compassion and love to help you; and believe me; you've done a lot for me, as well." Veronica picked up Ryan, giving him a hug.

"And so the legacy of the cedar chest goes on. Ryan, in turn, will be blessed, and pass his good fortune to the next one that God has waiting for him; whether it be his child, or another person in need," Ben added.

"That's right, Dad. Who knew a beat-up old cedar chest could mean such much in the scheme of life."

"God, did, honey. He knew all along what it would take to bring us together again."

"And now we are a real family, the way God intended," she sighed.

"Yes. I've never heard a truer statement," Ben hugged her and she knew, at that very moment, she'd never loose him again.

REFLECTIONS

Living with family members, who suffer from bipolar disorder, or any other mental disease, is not an easy task, especially for children, who are unable to fully understand that they are the innocent victims, and not the root of the problem. However, there is a light at the end of that dark tunnel.

I developed the following list of questions and reflections to help you navigate this emotional rollercoaster, while you walk with God on your journey to find your true self.

Use them as a meditation, guidelines, or as a venue to ask God to heal your wounded soul, which will lead to the forgiveness of those who wounded you.

1. Veronica's name means 'true face or true identity'. Sometimes facing ourselves is painful and out of fear, or as a self—defense mechanism we hide behind different masks. **Make a list of the masks which you need to hand over to God so He can reveal your true self.**

2. **Think of a series of unfortunate events in your life and evaluate how you dealt with them.** Write your answer below each question that applies to you.

• Did you ask God for assistance and trusted in His mysterious ways and timing?

• Did you try dealing with them on your own, ending with standing alone at a dead–end street?

• Did you even try to block and hide them in an obscure corner of your memory denying their existence?

1. Veronica's perception of her parents and Uncle Jeb, was warped by her abusive childhood, and to cope with her dysfunctional family dynamic, she made a list of reasons to rationalize each person's behavior. However, none of her assumptions were based on the truth. Can you identify with Veronica's warped perception of her relationships?

2. **Take an inventory of each situation in your life. Were your assessments not based in truth, but rather in emotions? Hand them over to God and say a prayer for clearing your perspective and for revealing the truth to you in His perfect timing.**

3. Veronica harbored anger, which colored her vision of good people and their motives. What does the Bible say about anger and forgiveness? **Ask God to help you find all the scriptures that deal with anger and forgiveness which apply to your unique circumstances. Pray on each one, listen to God's message to you and write it down for further meditation. Next, make a list of people you need to forgive: (either living or deceased; friend, family member, co-worker, relative) Pray to God for guidance and healing of your heart, as He shows you how to**

handle each situation. If helpful, write each one a letter, you need not mail it, unless you believe you should.

4. Veronica's mother's illness caused her to be verbally abusive to her daughter. Once the truth was revealed, and Veronica analyzed the facts from a different point of view, she was able to make amends with her mother. After forgiveness, the healing process began. The next time someone comes at you in a hurtful manner, ask God to help you see that person through His eyes, so you could see the truth behind the assault, and be able to act in a forgiving manner. Don't be afraid to ask God to show you were harsh words or criticism has colored your perception of yourself and others around you. Give each situation to God and wait on His actions.

• Children of abuse find it hard to trust other human beings. If you have problems dealing with this issue, ask God to help you find people you can trust to help you through your trust issues.

- If you believe a child has been verbally or physically abused do not ignore it and turn the other way. Report your suspicions to your priest, pastor, or a trustworthy person in authority, assured they will take action and do the right thing for the child and the family.

- Study the Bible and find all the passages dealing with God's protection and love. List them and use it to help someone or yourself who is struggling with fear and matters of trust. Memorize those Bible verses and recite them out loud when you feel trapped or distrustful, if you're sure that those feelings come out of fear and not from a legitimate reason to distrust.

Now that you have done the hard work, keep the scriptures at hand and use them frequently to keep you grounded. Review your answers to the above questions often and ask God to help you with it.

AFTERWORD

Children who grow up in households where there is bipolar disorder, believe they are the cause of the unhappiness. A child cannot understand what they have done to cause so much emotional and verbal abuse. In other words, why is Daddy or Mommy so angry with me? Why am I not wanted or loved?

As a result, they blame themselves, believing they are bad children and worthless. Often these feelings of worthlessness carry into adulthood, manifesting themselves in various destructive ways.

If you need support or information on the disorder, don't be ashamed to get help. Check with your local mental health agencies. Speak to your pastor or priest, often times they can refer you to a place(s) that can help.

Above all, trust in God.

Many Blessings,
Angela Pisaturo

Lightning Source UK Ltd.
Milton Keynes UK
UKHW03n0227070418
320635UK00002B/7/P